Hunted

Published by

Two Realms Publishing LLC

https://tworealmspublishingllc.com

Book Cover: We Got You Covered Book Design

Interior Design: Two Realms Publishing LLC

Editor: Ink It Out Editing & Michelle's Edits

ISBN: 978-1-955106-46-7

1st edition 2025

Author's Note

This is kind of a warning, but not the
kind you're thinking of.

Or that I normally give.

If you're like me and you enjoy a
chronological reading order, then here it is.

Be forewarned, you will have to jump to
another series and well, things get brutal and
dirty (the good kind, as well as the bad) in
there. They might get a little bloody here, too.

Blood Sacrifice
Hunted
Rebel Tides (Prisma Isle™ 3)
Siren's Curse (Prisma Isle™ 4)
Silencing the Shape Shifter (Prisma Isle™ 5)
Kingdom of Embers (Prisma Isle™ 6)

Then back to this series.

Hunted

THE ATLIS CHRONICLES

A PRISMA ISLE™ SERIES SPIN-OFF

BOOK ONE

KRYS FENNER

TWO REALMS PUBLISHING LLC

City of the Perished (Ruins)
Windborn
Cragst
The Deep Abyss (Caves)
Blindpass
Bardaris
Jandal

Silverspire
Arradan
Realm
of Bahalah
Khobala

The Atlis Chronicles

Blood Sacrifice

Prisma Isle™

Perfectly Reckless

Chaotic Tranquility

Rebel Tides

Terminology

Atlis: an offshoot of the sirens created by Demeter, but with far more power, the ability to jump between realms and planes, and one purpose: to serve the gods and goddesses and helping those who cannot help themselves

Allimos: the soulmate of an Atlis

An Talamh Lus: The Plant Land

Babian(s): a creature with an ape-like appearance that is covered head-to-toe in fur and walks upright on two feet

Catalync: pronounced cat-ah-link; lynx-like creature with blue-gray fur and spiked tail that serves as a guide to Guardhians (part of the crossover from The Guardhian Series)

Collector: a position denoted by one of *The Divine Trinity* for those who possess the strength necessary to capture members from the Opposition

Draconis: a tall creature with a forked tongue, covered in dragon-scales who has a thick tail, typically ranging from 4-6 feet in length

Drokar: a two-headed hound that spits fire and has several tentacles coming out of its body

Guardian: any creature/man/woman/person charged with the protection of another who holds significant value

Guardhian: a person/creature with power used for guarding one of nine realms created by the gods (part of the crossover from The Guardhian Series)

Hunter: a position denoted by one of *The Divine Trinity* for those whose tracking skills far exceed the others

Mammolisk: this is a large beast with rows of sharp teeth, a leathery hide, long black claws, and spikes along its spine and tail

Mutuphin: the species created by the goddess, Luna; this creature has sea-foam green skin, a slender build, large wings, antennae, long tails, and no identifiable gender

Prohtector: a person/creature who aids and protects Guardhians (part of the crossover from The Guardhian Series)

The Divine Trinity: the name of the coven of Warlocks, typically identified by the three-pointed star embedded in one's forehead

Yokai: a demonic animal with dark scales, a large maw, and razor-sharp teeth

One

How the fuck do I get out of this? Thalasia thought as she pressed her back against the cold stone. A low rumble resounded nearby as she surveyed the barren wasteland in front of her. It was arid and dusty, completely desolate. Nothing but one empty home after another caught her eye. No true means of escape from the massive creature that lumbered in her direction. Its long black claws and the spikes covering its leathery hide presented an enormous issue. Peering around the side, the creature lifted its large maw into the air and sniffed, obviously seeking her out.

This couldn't be where her vision had meant to take her. Except, the portal she'd traveled through led her to a set of ruins. How was she supposed to find a young siren here? One problem at a time. First, she had to locate a good hiding spot either amidst the stone huts that still stood or in the piles of rubbish resembling rotting animal carcasses.

The creature snorted and chuffed, following some kind of invisible trail as it circled by a grime-covered window she'd eyeballed not three minutes back. Shit. Had it caught her scent? Of course. Naturally, it used something she hadn't masked all that well. Scanning one thatched roof to another, she searched for an escape route from the quiet village. This place hadn't offered her much of anything regarding information. All she'd noticed was layer upon layer of sand coating what furniture filled the empty houses.

From what little she saw in front of her; only one escape option presented itself—the skies.

Thalasia glanced toward the scorching sun. It was now or never. Tucking her wings back, she crouched down low on her haunches. A gust of wind whipped through the village, knocking loose a strand of blue hair from the scarf around her head. The creature roared. The earth shook as it charged toward her. Thalasia all but launched into the air. Its jaws snapped, almost getting her within its grasp.

The hairs on the nape of her neck remained at full attention, even as she soared higher, flying through the cloudless desert sky. Her wings flapped with great effort, propelling herself forward with every ounce of strength she possessed. It was the only way she would leave that creature behind. Not that she knew anything about it, let alone how fast it ran. At least this way, it couldn't trail her scent.

Refusing to look back, Thalasia focused all of her energy on the blue-glass clarity before her. There was no telling how she flew overhead before she scanned the sea of sand below, searching for any sign of life. Or even a place to hide and spend the night. Nothing. The vast, bone-dry basin offered her nothing except the heat beating down on her wings.

Unable to sustain flight any longer, she landed with the grace of a peacock. The soles of her boots scraped across the sand as her feet hit the ground. Her wings had dried out in the thick heat. Usually, she kept the siren appearance because it made her look like less of a threat. In this weather, she didn't think it benefited her.

Gods, how long had she been in the sky? Eyeing the position of the sun once more, she guesstimated at least a couple of hours. If only she could determine how far she'd gotten since departing the village. It all looked the same. This kind of terrain didn't suit her body. Thalasia wiped the sweat from her brow, and with the flick of her hand, she adjusted her overall appearance so she looked human. She rolled her wingless shoulders and adjusted the brown scarf around her head so it covered her mouth. Damn, that felt much better. Now, if she could locate civilization somewhere in this realm of endless rolling foothills, that would be great.

The day had worn on. No matter how many slopes she'd climbed and descended, she'd gotten no closer to another village. Bahalah had to have something to offer her. Thalasia's silver gaze flicked briefly to the sun. It would set soon. A slight chill swept through her. She needed to find shelter somewhere. There was no telling what other creatures wandered these dunes throughout the night. Once the sun dipped below the horizon, only the inhabitants of this realm knew the treachery that would slip away into the shadows. Halting her steps, she took a moment to settle her ragged breaths and scan the horizon. Her eyes landed on another dune not faraway, except it was off somehow.

It appeared taller and yellower than what she'd seen thus far. Maybe it wasn't a grouping of dunes at all, but something else entirely. A gust of wind howled, yanking a few strands of her hair free from the scarf around her face. Her silver eyes narrowed as she stared at the collection of formations ahead. It looked—another prolonged cry of the wind resounded. Except it was far too close to just be the surrounding atmosphere. She whipped her head in the direction it had come from. "Shit," Thalasia muttered. Without a second to waste, she darted for that rocky landscape.

There was no other choice. Somehow, that damn creature from the village had caught up with her. Sand kicked up beneath her feet with every step she took. The closer she got to the bramble, the easier it became to discern that it held something within its confines. A small cavern, perhaps. Or even something more extensive. Either way, it offered shelter and a place to hide.

Or so she hoped.

Despite her preference, she lacked the time for the careful navigation of the twisted shrubbery and entry into the cave. She barreled forward, barely crossing its cold threshold when the thundering sounds of galloping reached her ears. As dark as it was in the cave, normally she'd retrieve a flashlight from the small bag hanging at her waist. But that would only draw further attention from the creature. Thankfully, she could see well enough without aid. Humans didn't exactly have her eyesight. Not that she even knew if this realm had humans. She should've scoured the book before hitting a jump point.

Moving deeper into the cave, Thalasia kept her footsteps as quiet as possible. She didn't need that *thing* following her in here. Though how the hell had it tracked her to begin with? Her scent? But shit. Given the distance she'd covered, that should've been next to impossible. Biting back a groan, she scrubbed a hand down her face. Definitely needed to read the book.

Winding around the stalagmites protruding from the floor, she eyeballed the bumpy stone walls. Her ears twitched. Something was there. Not that she could see it, let alone identify it, but it hadn't attacked her. Surveying the walls, she noted slight changes in their coloration and formation, how they shifted with the diminishing sunlight from the cave's entrance. It might help her locate whatever hid in the cavern, watching her. Running her fingers down the jagged edges of the stone barrier, she sensed it was nearby, but how close? "I know you're there."

Unable to determine if it was friend or foe, she discreetly settled her hand on the blade's hilt tucked into the back of her pants. "I'm not here to hurt you." Although it was the truth, none of them ever initially believed her. Not that she understood why. She didn't look threatening. Did she? No matter. She had to figure out what had happened at this place. The success of her mission depended on it.

Thalasia skimmed her fingertips along a vein of quartz as she strode forward. Still nothing. No subtle movements for her ears to pick up. No differentiation of color against the walls that she observed. One slight flutter and she'd know which way to look. "I'm here to help, but the longer you hide, the less of a reason I have to trust you want life to improve."

The sound of paws thudding against the sand echoed off the walls, halting Thalasia in her steps. *Damn it*, she thought to herself. That thing hadn't just caught up with her; it must've picked up her scent. Like a damn bloodhound. She scanned the cavern. There had to be a way to cover her scent. If only she knew how to kill it, then she'd fight, but it was far too late to search the book. And whatever hid here wasn't any damn help.

Sand covered the floor and the ceiling. As much as she loathed the idea of giving some of her abilities away like this, no other choice presented itself. Summoning her power, Thalasia shifted the terrain, gently eased more grains to the entrance, and coated her body in it. Gods, this sucked. She pressed tight against the wall, listening intently to its movements.

A slim, tall body cloaked hers. Something long and curved came over her mouth. "Shh. Be quiet."

What the fuck was this thing? She'd seen some doozies in her life, all fifteen years, but nothing like *this*. It had *no* hair. At least it appeared that way. It was difficult to tell with its green skin. If nothing else, at least the creature had a mouth. One that barked out orders like a king. Or queen. She couldn't tell. Not that it mattered. Though it would've been great if it had given her a chance to respond before covering her mouth with… what the fuck had it used? An extra limb?

This creature was definitely unlike anything she'd ever seen before. Something this realm seemed to have in spades. And it made the situation even more perilous, especially if they had to escape for any reason. Did it really think her mouth was the problem? Like she required it to... enchant? Internally groaning, Thalasia pressed her head back against the hard stone. *For fuck's sake, please don't tell me you sent me somewhere full of witches and warlocks.*

No response.

As if she expected less. Yeah, the gods could give her painful visions, but a conversation was always out of the fucking question.

The sand vibrated underfoot, the earth quaked, and a low growl announced the beast lumbering toward them. Grit kicked up in its wake, showering down on them. The creature snorted and chuffed, lifting its large nostrils and flicking its massive tongue into the air as if it were trying to source out their scents. Its leathery chest heaved with each breath, circling the cave, tracking and retracing her steps in an endless loop.

Thalasia remained still, holding a bout of oxygen in her lungs. She didn't give a shit how much they burned. She refused to even let out a shallow breath until that thing left. Despite all her abilities in her arsenal, she didn't have a clue what would destroy the massive creature. Between what she and the thing pressed against her had done, hopefully it proved enough to keep them safe. Her silver gaze swung toward the back of the cavern. There was no discernible exit, which meant they'd have to create one if it came down to it.

Yeah, great place to hide.

Whose brilliant idea was this again?

The beast grunted, shaking its enormous head and spiked body. Its ragged breaths ruffled the hairless creature's antennae. Her brows dipped low, studying more of the thing holding her back as the beast exited the cave. Thalasia didn't release the breath she'd held until she heard the animal's paws leading away from the entrance. Oh, thank the gods. It must've assumed she'd taken to the skies just as she'd done last time to evade its grasp.

Thalasia scrunched her nose as she focused on the thing in front of her. Its slim, genderless figure, sea foam-colored skin, and large wings reminded her of something. But what? Her eyes widened as it hit her. *A Luna moth!* Except it was much bigger than an ordinary part of nature.

More man-sized. Taller than her. And she had already hit her full height of five-eight. Still, it looked strange. That was saying something, as she had invisible wings.

Silence stretched between her and the moth-like creature as it continued holding her back. Like it believed the monster might just return. After another beat or two, perhaps longer, it spoke, its voice similar to a gentle caress of the wind. "I'm going to release you. Once I do, you'll be wise to put away your weapon."

Weapon? What the fuck was it talking about? Thalasia tilted her head as the creature's tail left her mouth. Yep. Tail. Fuck, this world was making her head spin. Shaking some sense into her gray matter, she narrowed her gaze. Aside from her powers, it could only have referenced one thing. "You mean my knife?" Taking her cue from the creature, she kept her voice low. Obviously, it knew more about the beast than she did. "What was that thing?"

"A blade is a weapon. Is it not?" Its pale eyes assessed her as it stepped back, putting a small bit of space between them. "You're a sorceress, you should know."

"A sorceress?" Thalasia scoffed. That was a new one. "I've been called a lot of things, but never a witch." With a slight shake of her head, she unwrapped the scarf from her face, pushed off the wall, and dropped the glamour that hid her blue-feathered wings. Rolling her shoulders, she stretched them wide and then tucked them back. Ah, much better.

Its pale eyes darted from the end of one wing to the other, scrutinizing each part of her plumage as if she had somehow tricked it. The corner of its mouth lifted slightly as it cocked its head at her. "You're a siren, but... different."

In more ways than one. Not that she offered any further details regarding that matter. It wasn't something she shared. At all.

The creature's forehead wrinkled, its antennae curling a bit as it clasped its hands together. "Instead of leading with your intentions, or lack there-of, offer details regarding your plan to help. It's more diplomatic, less acrimonious."

Except diplomacy didn't always work. In her experience, it usually land-ed her in more trouble. Probably because she didn't pretty things up. Among other things. "As I don't know what happened here, hard to say how I can help. So, how about we try this? You answer a question and I'll answer one."

"I'm amenable to that, but first we should take to the sky before the mammolisk catches your scent on the wind and resumes the hunt."

Without giving her a chance to respond, the creature tucked its wings back, took off through the opening, and darted into the sky. "Sure, why not," Thalasia muttered, rolling her eyes. At least it gave her one piece of information. Now, if she could just figure out how to kill the mammolisk, all would be right. Striding forward, she launched into the velvety-black night sky filled with glittering stars and a glowing moon.

Quietly, they soared over the endless sea of rolling foothills and vast canyons. As they flew along, she scanned the dunes below, eyeing the wildlife that came alive at night. Although she appreciated the drop in temperature, nothing spectacular stood out to her. Wait. What the fuck was that? Did it have horns? Alright. Maybe this realm had something unique to it.

Unable to stand the silence any longer, she peered at the moth-like creature next to her. "Where exactly are we going?" It would be great if she had more than just a snippet of information. Maybe even a name to go with this creature. Or what it was. That would be good to know, too.

"A sanctuary," it called out.

That was good. So to speak. Her version of a sanctuary was likely different from theirs. As long as it was safe. That was all that mattered. Besides, the more she knew, the easier she could determine their next steps. "What happened to this place? The village back there?"

"Warlocks. And their collectors."

"You mean that beast? You called it a mammolisk, right?" She needed to dig into her book once they settled. Any insight it could provide would be helpful.

"No." Its antennae furrowed. "The mammolisk are hunters answering their master's call. They're destructive, however, simple threats compared to those in power."

"Alright, so killing the beast doesn't necessarily stop them." Great. She'd arrived a short time ago, and already she had more than one problem. "What are the collectors?"

Growing quiet, the creature came to a halt, and she followed suit. It stared at her, once again assessing her. "What business could a girl your age possibly have alone in the desert, running from forces she holds no knowledge of, much less comprehends?"

A girl her age, yeah, she got that a lot. It didn't matter how much she'd lost in her short life. All that mattered was her mission. Details of which she couldn't provide, but she had to give the creature something. Thalasia swallowed the lump in the back of her throat. "I don't pick the place, I just go where the gods send me," she blurted. What in the actual fuck? That wasn't what she meant to say. The words tumbled out of her mouth before she could stop them.

"You don't strike me as the type to follow orders."

Tell that to the pain that occurred if she didn't heed her visions. "Despite what you believe, I'm here to help. The golden siren is in danger. It's my job to save her." Why the fuck was she telling it all of this? This wasn't how she typically handled things. Despite every effort to offer some semblance of an honest answer, she couldn't seem to execute the right words.

"Save her?"

Shit. Thalasia scrubbed her hand across her face. She'd already stepped in it. Since she'd opened her mouth, might as well put it all out there. "Yes. I've seen it. She's somewhere dark and cold." It wasn't much to go on, but her versions never gave her a lot to begin with. "I went to the village searching for information. You're right; I'm not a siren. I'm an Atlis. It's my job to go from world to world rescuing those who need it." That seemed like an oversimplification, but she refused to acknowledge all of life's complexities.

The steady beat of its wings threw small gusts, though hardly noticeable. Its pale eyes narrowed. "Yes, you've made the *rescue* part clear, but what do you mean? Rescue who? The golden siren?"

The pitch of its voice heightened. As if her words had somehow spooked it. Which made no sense. Hadn't she been succinct? How did it not understand—danger, dark and cold? Maybe if she broke this down a little more. "Correct. Whoever she is, she isn't at the sanctuary. I don't know where she is, only that she's a prisoner. Though you've mentioned warlocks, so I'd say they likely have her. If you require more on the how, well, I need more information to formulate a plan. Any more questions?"

Without so much as a word, it bolted, taking off in the direction they'd been traveling. Not that words were necessary. The speed at which it flew told her everything. And nothing. But Thalasia didn't hesitate to chase after the green, mothy creature. It had all the answers she required to save the golden siren. Maybe even the realm. She might just have to salvage one to get to the other. Not the first time that had happened.

Nor likely the last.

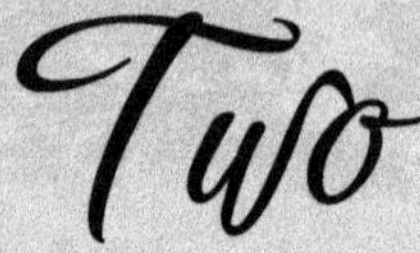

urmoyes dove toward what constituted the central part of the sanctuary. They cared little whether or not the blue siren trailed behind. They had far larger concerns. Scanning the settlement, they narrowed their pale eyes. Something was wrong. Pots appeared overturned. Mud bricks looked scattered about. They flew down, landing on the earth with graceful ease. Nearby inhabitants picked up various items littering the ground. "What happened?"

No one answered.

Not that it was necessary. Given the fragmented homes and other objects in disarray, either a mammolisk, a hunter, or a collector had found them. Something that seemed inanely impossible. The sanctuary was well-hidden. At least, it should have been. A large, rocky landscape surrounded Blindpass, fortifying the city. Of all the towns, it was the only haven remaining. Out of their periphery, they spotted the blue siren's landing. She executed it nearly as perfectly as their own, her feet hitting the dry earth like that of a gazelle, light and airy.

"Where are we?" the female demanded.

"Somewhere safe." In theory. Striding forward, they eyed their environs, attempting to determine which of their enemies had located the sanctuary. As well as searched for either the leader or Adoni. The blue-winged creature followed along, trailing after them, spouting off one question after another. Not that they paid the female much mind, even as they stopped to aid members of the resistance here and there. The townspeople offered little information regarding the situation at hand.

From what they'd seen, it had to be a mammolisk. Those monstrosities had excellent olfactory senses. They could catch the scent of any creature miles away. Their pale gaze swung around and fell onto an almost completely decimated hut just beyond the clearing and the teenager helping an older male with the pickup. "Urbi," Nurmoyes stated as they approached.

The young, dark-haired male's gaze lifted from the brick in his hands. A chilling glint reflected in his sapphire eyes. He tossed the clay rectangle aside and closed the little distance between them. "Where have you been? We could've used you here!"

It served no purpose to recount how they'd found themselves in the Deep Abyss. Or how they wound up bringing someone back from those cavernous trenches. Urbi would sight the female soon enough. Nurmoyes folded their arms across their chest. "What happened here?"

"A hunter and one of its pets. We're not sure how they located us, but we think they may have tracked a villager on a water trek." Urbi frowned, gripping a handful of his black hair. "We fought back hard. Our preparations helped. Still, they injured several of our fighters, but we chased them off."

Chased, not killed, Nurmoyes thought. "Where is Najjar? Adoni?"

"My mother is in the infirmary, tending to the wounded." The boy's brows drew tightly together. "I don't know about Adoni, though. She might be with her."

"I shall check." That child was their responsibility. Pivoting on their heel, they glowered at the blue-winged siren and pointed to the hut. "Stay here and help him."

"What? No, I need answers. How am I supposed to get—"

"You will get them when I am ready to provide them." Their pale gaze flicked to Urbi. "Watch her. Do not let her wander. Understood?"

Urbi's eyes widened as he stared at the blue-haired female. He visibly slumped his shoulders, he lowered his hand to almost touch the ground, and he fixed his gaze solely on her.

Nurmoyes snapped their fingers. "Urbi!"

He shook his head, snapping out of a momentary daze. "Uh, yeah. I can do that."

Ah, yes, the natural effect sirens had on the opposite sex. Though she wasn't fully siren, was she? Still, it seemed that much applied to her. Urbi had responded much the same way with Adoni, and she had just turned thirteen. It had something to do with their enchantment powers. Something Nurmoyes never understood. Without another word, Nurmoyes jogged deeper into the village, ignoring the blue siren's calls that trailed after them. Her words got lost in the wind. They needed to find Adoni. Now. Not fret over or handhold the other female.

If the warlocks seized their ward, then all was lost.

And everything they fought for was over.

Thalasia's silver gaze narrowed, fixating on the moth-like creature as it took off with a soft fluttering sound. She was torn between despising two equally awful things. Being treated like an insolent child or disregarded as nothing more than a pebble in their non-existent shoe. With a grunt, she threw her hands up and focused on the dark-haired male standing there staring at her with a set of blue eyes, more intense than any she'd ever seen.

Why the hell hadn't he looked away yet? Did she have something on her face? Cheeks? Had she unknowingly drooled or something? A shiver ran down her spine, making the hair on the nape prickle with unease. He made her skin crawl. "Well?" When he didn't move or even respond, she waved a hand in front of his face. "Hello?" Did she have to knock on his forehead or some shit?

"What?"

"Are you going to tell me what you want me to do or continue gawking at me like a fish on a hook?" She could seriously do without the latter. The creature had saved her, or so she believed. For the time being, it made sense to follow its orders. Besides, this might be the opportunity she required to learn more about this realm. And her entire purpose for being here.

"Right. Sorry," the human muttered. Striding past her, his long legs ate up the distance between them and the battered structure. "We need to move the bricks into separate piles, salvaging whatever we can. If it is no longer usable, then it goes into the wheelbarrow for disposal."

"Simple enough." While she could likely move things along faster if she used her powers, this presented an opportunity. One she refused to pass up. Thalasia marched to one side, hefted an ashen-colored stone in her palms, and added it to a growing pile. Back and forth a few more times before she addressed any of her questions.

"I appreciate your help with this."

"Not like he gave me much of a choice." She knew little about this realm. Something that moth-like creature had taken full advantage of.

"They," the dark-haired male corrected.

Thalasia cocked an eyebrow at him and propped her hands on her hips. "Excuse me?"

"You're referring to Nurmoyes, right? They have no gender, so the term would be *they*."

No gender? How was that possible? Or was it a human thing? Possibly. Humans were strange. There was still a lot she didn't comprehend about them. Not that the creature shared any of their attributes, except for walking upright on two legs, but so did she. "Okay. They. And... I guess. They didn't give me their name."

"Well, Nurmoyes is their name. And I'm Urbi, and this is Dorak." He gestured to the elderly male working alongside them. "You are?"

It seemed harmless to produce her name. She'd given more to the creature. And if she didn't share it with Urbi, those keen, blue eyes of his told her this conversation would cease. Along with any hope of learning a damn thing about this place. "Thalasia."

The corner of Urbi's mouth lifted. "Welcome to Blindpass, Thalasia."

"Thanks, I think." As the two men returned to work, she surveyed the village. Homes built of sandstone, with open windows to catch the breeze. The bright orange flames crackled nearby, yet offered little light against the moon's silvery glow. A whistling wind stirred the canopies above small porches, outdoor seating areas, and a market stall brimming with fresh goods. Could this possibly be reminiscent of that one village's former appearance? Before it had all gotten destroyed? "What is this place, exactly? Nurmoyes called it a sanctuary, but from what?"

Urbi halted in his movements. His blue gaze swung in her direction. "The warlocks."

Fuck. Thalasia barely bit back a groan, scrubbing a hand down her face, silencing what escaped. The one thing she'd prayed against and it existed in this realm. Of fucking course. As if the gods would send her anywhere else. "And it's Nurmoyes job to protect this place? This haven?"

"No. The guardian helps us, yes, but their duty isn't to us."

She narrowed her eyes, a slight frown creasing her brow, and folded her arms tightly across her chest. What? That made no sense. Who were they bound to protect? Thalasia opened her mouth—

"You should not be telling her this," Dorak interjected. "Who is she to us? A stranger. No one we know."

"But Nurmoyes brought her here. They wouldn't have done that if we couldn't trust her."

"They also told you not to let her wander," the old male snapped.

"Did it ever occur to you that maybe I'm here to help? And that's why they brought me along?" she suggested. If they were going to dissect her like a specimen in plain sight, then let their whispers paint a gallery of outcomes, not just one looming doom. All of them rang true.

"Then why would they not say that?" Dorak demanded. "Hmm?"

Good point. Not that she'd admit it. Although... she cracked a toothy grin. "Because they know they haven't given me enough information, so I can advise *how* I can help."

The old-guy's eyes narrowed, his bushy eyebrows furrowing as he gave her a real once-over, like he didn't trust a word she said. He jabbed his forefinger at her. "I don't like you."

Thalasia rolled her eyes. *Take a number.* He wasn't the first and likely wouldn't be the last. No one approved of being told they'd done something wrong or of having *a child* come in to clean up their mess. "And?"

"Stop being rude, Dorak," Urbi snapped.

Hmm. Her hero. Not that she needed him to step up on her behalf or come to her defense. Though it certainly did the job. The old man's nose wrinkled as he muttered something under his breath about arrogant youngin's. Ah, yes, because age automatically meant experience. No way could she have lived five lifetimes of shit in her short fifteen years in this universe. Thalasia smirked. If only that were true.

Shaking his head, Urbi sighed. "So, you think you can help? How?"

"I can't answer that."

"Can't? Or won't?"

"Can't," she reiterated. If she could, she would. "I don't know what you all need to offer a proper response." That didn't mean they couldn't meet in the middle. Even if she had to propose it. Thalasia half-shrugged. "Why is this place necessary? Can you tell me that, and maybe I can give you something in return?"

The male cast a furtive glance at their surroundings, pausing briefly on the old man before landing on her. "It's our only way to fight against the hunters and collectors. To reclaim what the warlocks stole from us. Keep them from enslaving those of us who remain."

"Reclaim?"

With a rough swipe of his thumb across his sweaty forehead, Urbi frowned, crossing his arms. "This is our last haven. We had others, but the warlocks with their... disciples overtook them, killing the guardians and golden sirens, and enslaving our people."

"When I advised I would provide her answers when I was prepared to do so, did you assume it was your duty to offer them?" Nurmoyes asked as they approached, with a dark-haired female at their side.

Urbi gripped the back of his neck. "Well, no, but I just thought... you know, it couldn't hurt?"

Nurmoyes clasped their hands at the small of their back. "I would contend the opposite. It could cause irreparable harm. Given how little we know of her, Adoni's absence, and the knowledge she seems to have regarding such."

"I get it. You don't trust me," Thalasia inserted. The feeling was mutual. Not that it was a luxury she could afford. "What if I can give you something that might help with that?"

"Such as?" the female questioned.

Focusing on her, Thalasia studied the features of the newcomer. Jet-black hair. Her bright, sapphire-blue eyes, ever vigilant, swept the environment, as if cataloging every detail. A slightly angular nose. All the features that Urbi shared. This had to be his mother. Not that she recalled the name referenced. Nor did it immediately matter. The rest of what she remembered about that part of the conversation did. It gave her a way in. "You have wounded, right? I could heal them, and if you'll allow me, I could help take back some of your lost villages."

The woman cocked her head as her eyebrows lowered. "You can heal them?"

Her mouth twitched. Yeah, she understood the female's wariness. If she wasn't, well... her, she wouldn't believe her, either. That didn't mean she couldn't prove them wrong. "Hey, Urbi. Give me your hand?" Thalasia requested, adding a slight lilt to her tone. Not that she required the help, but best not to chance it.

"Sure."

As he marched over to her and extended his arm, she discreetly palmed a stone with a sharpened edge from the rubble. "This might hurt." With the snap of her wrist, she sliced open the meaty pad of his thumb until the blush of red bloomed. Perfect. She tossed the rough rock aside, her hand hovering just above his calloused palm. From the jagged wound poured silver light, humming with a faint energy. Delving deep into the veins, it healed with a soft, pulsing light, stitching the skin back together as if the cut hadn't occurred. Grinning widely, Thalasia tilted her chin, indicating Urbi's hand with a subtle nod. "Like it's brand new." Her gaze lifted to his. "Go ahead. Give it a whirl."

The woman's blue eyes widened as she came over and jerked Urbi's palm out of Thalasia's hold. Lifting his calloused hand, she twisted and turned it around, inspecting every part of Urbi's thumb, searching for answers. Her gaze flicked to Thalasia. "How did you do this?"

Talk about a complicated answer. How much did she explain? Did she go into the creation of the Atlis? That went against the rules. And she'd already delved way too much to Nurmoyes. It didn't matter if it was unintentional. She'd still done it. But she couldn't let this go, either. She had to give them something. Perhaps an oversimplification? In a way, they would understand. "Magic. Not unlike what your warlocks possess, but different."

"You are a sorceress," Nurmoyes interjected. "As previously addressed."

Thalasia scoffed. Not that simple. "No, I'm not. Yes, I have magical powers, but unlike... the warlocks,"—because it was the only example she had—"I don't use my abilities to torture. Like I told you, I can heal your soldiers if you'll allow me and help you retake the villages stolen from you."

Her silver gaze swung to the female, who appeared to be in charge in some capacity. "You're human. You need someone who can fight against the warlocks and their regime."

Before Nurmoyes could intercede, the female raised her hand, cutting them off. "She's right. However, we don't know you or what you are capable of, aside from what you've demonstrated. So, heal our soldiers, as long as you don't have to hurt them to do it."

"I don't." It was just the easiest way to prove her point. Thalasia held out her hand, offering what she hoped the woman would accept. Silence stretched between them as the female's blue gaze scrutinized her proposal. Finally, she clasped Thalasia's outstretched palm. They shook. "Good. If you'll lead the way."

"Of course."

At least something had gone in the right direction. It was a small step, but she had to start somewhere. Hopefully, nothing else derailed her from her ultimate mission.

Failure wasn't an option.

Adoni groaned as her eyes slowly fluttered open. Chains clinked as she lifted a hand to rub her throbbing head. What in the world? What happened? Where was she? Why couldn't she see anything? Lightly touching the left side of her face, Adoni hissed. The area around her eye hurt. It seemed swollen. Not that she could recall how it occurred.

Maybe it would come to her. First, she needed to figure out where she was. Her brown gaze swung left and then right from one stone wall to the next. Filthy straw lay scattered across the dirt floor. She eyed the iron wrapped tightly around both of her wrists. Pushing to her feet, she eyed the short steel bars high on the wooden door across the way. At least that answered one question. She was in a dungeon of some kind.

But where?

Tugging on the chain links, she tried to spread her wings, which got her nowhere, and attempted to get closer to the door to peer through what constituted a window. Except she couldn't get close enough to see anything. The iron wouldn't go that far. She needed a rock or brick or something to break these things. The flickering flames of the torches offered little light. Aside from a bucket and a heap of clothing scraps, there wasn't anything she could use.

A set of heavy footsteps approached. Adoni inched backward as the entrance opened with a click and a clank. Her brown gaze leveled on the tall male striding forward. A predatory gleam entered his golden eyes as they narrowed on her. The hair on the nape of her neck stood at attention. She'd run if she could. Even fly far away. He'd left the passage wide open. But she froze, rooted to where she stood. As he closed the short distance between them, reaching out toward her, Adoni caught sight of the tri-star embedded in his forehead.

A warlock.

The male's calloused hand hovered inches from her chest. A rich, yellow light shimmered between them. A jolt of sharp pain made her gasp, sweat now slicking her forehead. "No!" Adoni screamed.

"What are you doing?" another male hollered.

With a snarl, the man dropped his hand and glanced over his shoulder. "What we should've done from the start."

Clutching her breast, Adoni staggered backward and nearly tripped over her wings. Her breath was a desperate, silent plea for air, a frantic struggle against the tightening pressure. A cold knot tightened in her throat, stealing the air from her lungs, as she fought to stay upright. The two men continued arguing back and forth.

"*She* is our last chance!"

"I'm aware of that."

"Yet, you were trying to forgo everything we've worked for so you could have a little extra juice?"

"Yes! Because that maggot has set us on a path that will never come to fruition."

"Not if you take her power before it has fully formed."

My power? That glow that had streamed between them. Her chest grew tight, a crushing weight stealing her breath as darkness crept at the edge of her vision. Was that what they'd done to all the others? Adoni eyed the two males. They both had the same pointed ears, three-pointed stars embedded in their foreheads, and the same amber-colored eyes. The one who'd assaulted her had cropped, white hair, while the other had long gray hair, partially worn back.

"We have a situation," a younger, male voice echoed down the hall.

Both warlocks exited. The one lingered in the jamb and stared at her hungrily. "You've gotten a reprieve. For today." With that, he left, locking her back inside the dungeon.

"And?"

"There was a ripple in the continuum several hours ago."

"Do we know what caused it?"

"No."

"*This* is why you can't have her," one male snapped. "I suggest you find out. And from now on, you stay away from here. We didn't grab her for nothing."

Three sets of footsteps resounded as all three males disappeared down the corridor. All of Nurmoyes's warnings replayed in her mind, but she hadn't listened. She'd insisted on proving useful to Najjar. Look where they got her. Adoni surveyed what little her prison held. No matter what, she couldn't end up like all the other golden sirens. She had to escape.

Before they could steal her power.

Three

As the flames crackled, Nurmoyes watched, feeling their heat as they reached up into the inky night sky. If only the crackling fire could provide the answers they sought, their arduous fight might prove worthwhile. Nothing helped. The more they tumbled through all they'd learned, the further away the solution seemed.

"I figured by now, you'd realize that won't tell you anything," Najjar stated.

They hadn't even heard her approach. "I should have been here for Adoni," they sighed heavily. If they hadn't gone out, then they could've prevented all of this. Including their latest arrival. Something they still didn't know what to do with.

"You cannot blame yourself."

"On that, we agree," Nurmoyes retorted. "The fault lies with you."

Najjar's blue gaze narrowed at them. "I told you on multiple occasions we needed better security, as well as addressing Adoni's age. She tried many times to get you to allow her to do something. Anything rather than become a burden, which is how she felt."

"How would you know that?"

"Because she talked to me."

"I am her guardian. She was... is my responsibility." Focusing back on the glow of the orange-and-red flames, they placed their hands behind their back and gripped one of their wrists. How could they not have seen this?

Adoni hadn't just required attention; she needed purpose. Something that didn't include hiding.

"Your duty to her isn't over. The warlocks need her alive. And you have someone who also needs your help and may serve as the solution you've been seeking all these years."

For now, at least. They'd never determined how long the warlocks kept the others alive before consuming their powers. What they had spent their life trying to stop. As had all the other guardians. Each had failed in their mission. "I do not trust her."

"Do you not recall what she did for us earlier? How she aided our soldiers? Something she didn't have to do."

"I have not forgotten. However, there are still too many unknowns." Where had the female come from? How could she look like a siren, yet have capabilities beyond that? Then again, that one, they had their suspicions. The same was true of Adoni.

"You mean you haven't gotten her to answer all your questions?" Najjar retorted. "I didn't think that was possible."

Nurmoyes peered at the female. It wasn't, but they hadn't used their powers on her since their first meeting, either "You have made your point."

"Then why are you still standing out here? Go find out what you want to know, because I can't tell you everything, but I can tell you that girl is special."

Of course, she could. Najjar was human, but she had what they called a gut feeling. Something that hadn't always steered them wrong over the years. Nurmoyes eyed the hut where they had placed Thalasia for the night. Their gaze once again returned to the fire. "I will. Shortly." Once they'd come up with a plan. One that worked for all parties involved.

A cool gust of wind swirled through the room, kicking up dust and grit in its wake. The thin pages of the journal fluttered. Thalasia gently slapped her hand down, stilling the paper's movement. She turned the lantern's light up a notch, focusing on the various journal entries. If anyone had come here before, she imagined it was her parents. That didn't mean another Atlis couldn't have held that luxury. Her line had existed for thousands of centuries. Nothing she'd skimmed over prior to their notes suggested that was the case.

Thalasia rubbed her chest. No matter how hard she tried, the tightness refused to loosen. She hated going through their passages. It brought back too many memories. Things she preferred not to think about. Especially on a night like tonight. She swallowed, trying to free the constriction in her throat. Fuck. Where had all the air gone? Why couldn't she get any oxygen into her lungs?

Jumping to her feet, Thalasia tossed the journal aside and stalked across the room to the open window. A chill shot down her spine as she stared at the night sky as if it could calm the tension coursing through her veins. The array of twinkling stars covering that inky, black abyss offered her nothing more than an endless sea of emptiness. Despite its clear visibility, it held no answers or solutions to the problems weighing heavily on her shoulders.

That responsibility lay solely with the Atlis journal. She peered at the leather-bound book she'd carelessly left on her cot and scrubbed a hand down her face. It didn't matter how many years had passed; this never got easier. "Nothing worth doing is ever easy," Thalasia muttered.

Words her mother had repeated time and time again.

Inhaling and exhaling a deep breath, she returned her attention to the dark sky. Her fingers, clammy and shaking, barely grazed the golden chain, the lyre charm a cold weight against her frantic pulse. Whether she had the strength, she had to push through. That was the job. The role the Atlis played in the grand scheme of it all. To rescue those who couldn't save themselves. A duty that belonged to her and her alone.

The memory crashed over Thalasia like a wave, each drop a stinging reminder of what was lost; silent tears streamed down her face, tracing a path of grief.

"Do you see that collection of stars?" her mother pointed out to a small grouping of three high above where they lay.

"They're so faint."

"That's because they are a mirror of the human world on the other side of this one. If you look closely enough, you can always see their constellations just beyond the darkness."

Zeroing in on the velvety night sky, Thalasia studied what went past the obvious. She'd only seen Orion's Belt that one time with her mother. No matter how many times she'd searched for any of the human constellations again, they'd never appeared. At least, not in another realm. *Gods, I miss them.* Mourning the past wouldn't get her anywhere or accomplish anything. Clearing her throat, she brushed the wetness from her face. These people needed her. Even if they didn't yet recognize it. She strode back to the cot, reclaimed her seat, and cracked the leather-bound book open.

It wasn't as comfortable as other places she'd stayed, but she'd also had worse. The cool air rustling audibly through the room, brushing against her skin, helped immensely. Thalasia scanned through the pages, skimming over her mother's passages. Nothing stood out. This realm hadn't—she frowned at the sticky texture coating the outer edge of one sheet. "What the hell?"

Running her fingers across the tacky substance, Thalasia eyed the date on one side and then the other. With how every Atlis labeled their notes, there was no way to tell if anything was out of place or missing. No one identified them with a specific calendar date. The difference between realms was too astronomical to do so. Still, was she overlooking something? She inspected the paper, closer to the binding, giving it a slight nudge. The fused pages bowed. "Holy shit."

It was almost as if two bushes lay closely together, whispering secrets to one another. Thalasia retrieved her dagger from the nightstand and carefully inserted it between the pages. Taking her time, she wiggled the blade's straight edge back and forth until the sheets crackled into separation. The border ripped. "Shit." She hadn't meant for that to happen. Beggars couldn't be choosers.

Wasn't that how the adage went?

Thalasia's silver gaze swung to the right side of the journal. She eyed the three sketches in place. Each had one or two notes scribbled alongside it, but not much else. While she didn't recognize the bottom two images, the first was all too familiar. Large beast. Long black claws. Spikes over its back and tail. A single word accompanied it—mammolisk.

The other two drawings comprised much the same thing. The labels identified one as draconis, lizard-like in appearance with large nostrils, a forked tongue, and a long, spiked tail; and the other as babian, ape-like in appearance with fangs, covered in head-to-toe fur, both walking on two feet. Great. Something to look forward to. Neither offered any substantial information. Maybe the other side was different. Her gaze flicked to the left side of the book.

"Summer." With a groan, Thalasia dragged a weary hand down her face. "Really, Mom? That's how you start this?" Gods, she prayed the rest of these scribbles gave her more than that and read on.

> *I'm uncertain of the year. I believe the human equivalent is 1946. That is likely very different here in Bahalah, but I haven't determined how they count the passage of time. Despite the existence of humans and blending in with them, almost no one has spoken with us. They seem skeptical of outsiders. Or at least, me and my Allimos.*
>
> *Regardless, we've visited every village. The golden sirens, along with their guardians, are thriving. Their vast cityscape is booming. Humans, warlocks, witches, draconis, and babians alike seem to have welcomed them with open arms. Hmm. Maybe we haven't blended as well as we believed. Or the shift in magic in the realm has offered them something they didn't have before. Many years have passed since the golden sirens first arrived. Or so I was told.*
>
> *Very little information exists about how they got here. Simply that they did. I don't know what the gods expect us to do. All appears well in the realm. I'm positive things will continue in that direction. We're moving on tomorrow.*

"That's it?" She flipped back and forth, the crisp paper rustling between her fingers, ensuring no other pages had stuck. Nope. Nothing. Aside from some basic information, her mother hadn't given her squat. Running her hands through her hair, she glared at the passage as if more words would magically appear.

No change.

Shit.

Slamming the journal shut, Thalasia hopped off the narrow bed. As that hadn't proven useful, maybe the map would have something. It should've been completely updated by now. Closing in on the corner of the room, where the parchment hovered, she eyed the graphic details of Bahalah's landscape, or lack thereof, and crossed her arms. This couldn't be right.

Sand dunes and rocky formations appeared in various places, all checking out. Everything lined up from what she'd seen on the flight to Blindpass. Except for this settlement. How was that possible? How could the spires around the village exist, but the village itself didn't? That made no sense. Unless... her gaze flicked back to the journal lying on the cot.

Her mother would've at least created a map. Even if everything seemed fine. Did that mean this was how it all looked back then? Maybe. It didn't explain why it hadn't yet updated, reflecting how it all appeared today. Thalasia frowned. Maybe she'd input the wrong sequence. Summoning the symbols, she tried again.

And waited.

After several minutes of her studying the damn thing at a snail's pace, nothing happened. It floated in the air, unchanging. She'd done nothing wrong. Could something be blocking it? Could the warlocks? Was that even possible with a magical artifact? Fuck. Of all the probable outcomes regarding the map, this wasn't something her parents had ever shared. Maybe even considered. "Well, I guess this has to be handled the old-fashioned way."

Thalasia flicked her wrist. The parchment furled, sealing itself shut, and flew to the small, velvet pouch she'd left on the bed. She ran a hand through her long, blue hair, fisting a handful as if the grip could ease the frustration pounding in her ears. This was supposed to be a way for her to get answers. Not to end up with more questions.

Sighing heavily, she put the journal away on her way to the exit. Time for her and Nurmoyes to have an honest conversation. And come to an arrangement that satisfied them both. Or so she hoped.

Nurmoyes held the orange-and-red flickering lights in their sight. Unable to decide, they remained exactly where Najjar had left them several minutes ago. Yes, Najjar was right. That made this even more difficult. Thalasia could prove useful. She already had. But it also meant they were responsible for her. After what happened with Adoni, the other golden sirens, and their kithfolk, it seemed ill-advised.

Instead of seeking the blue-winged non-siren, that kept them locked in place. A solution and complexity all rolled into one. The slight hairs on the nape of their neck prickled. Narrowing their gaze, the guardian scanned the village. Nothing seemed—"What are you doing out here? Why are you not inside, as instructed?"

"I needed to talk to you," Thalasia retorted.

Before Nurmoyes could respond, a bell clanged loudly, sounding the alarm of a nearby threat. Their gaze shot toward the guard station. *Not possible.* They pointed back in the direction Thalasia had come. "Get back inside! Now!" Without giving her a chance to argue, they darted into the night sky as shutters drew closed, covering windows. The villagers knew what they had to do.

Having gotten hit once, no one would risk a second attack. All of them followed protocol. Fires got doused. Each inhabitant battened down, crawling beneath floorboards or camouflaging in dirt holes. Whatever it took to cover scents, that was what they did. In less than two minutes' time, this place would become a ghost-town.

Landing on the outer platform, Nurmoyes strode into the watchtower and followed the guard's line of sight. Not that they could see much of anything. Not even an outline. It all appeared the same—one rolling foothill after another. The guard wouldn't have sounded the warning if something hadn't drawn near. "Mammolisk?"

"Yes."

"How far out?"

"Sixteen hundred meters and approaching. It'll arrive in less than five minutes."

A stiff breeze swept across the back of their neck. Something rustled against the tower's wooden surface. No, it couldn't. Their stomach dropped as they shut their eyes. *Please, by the goddess Luna, tell me I'm wrong and the child heeded my command.*

"What's coming?" Thalasia asked.

A deep frown etched itself onto Nurmoyes's face as the guardian glared intensely at the female. "This is not what I directed you to do." Why couldn't she have just listened? Did she think they hadn't instructed her for her own safety? Or that their words didn't matter?

"I'm aware."

"Yet you failed to heed my order." They didn't have time for this. The longer this conversation went on, the closer the mammolisk drew. Nurmoyes faced Thalasia, gripping her by the upper arm.

Jerking free from their grasp, she smirked. "Yes, I did. As far as I can tell, there's a situation and you require assistance."

"This is not your responsibility." That luxury belonged to them. Not the likes of a child. No matter how capable that child appeared, they had to handle things, including the protection of this village and its inhabitants.

Thalasia's silver eyes narrowed at them. Drawing herself to her full height of five-eight, she lifted her chin and crossed her arms. "Either I'm the solution or the problem, but I can't be both. So, which is it?"

This teenager didn't just call into question their judgment, but their every decision, purporting the very heart of what they'd considered earlier. *Is she the solution? Or another problem?* Had they even given her the opportunity to prove either was true? No, they hadn't. Nurmoyes blew out a soft breath. "What do you suggest?"

Sidestepping them, the blue-haired female approached the edge of the tower and stared out toward the creature. Her eyebrows furrowed. "Single mammolisk. Moving fast. Hmm." She peered at them briefly. "The spires don't fully surround the village, do they?"

"No."

"Are there underground tunnels?"

"Yes." Where had the female's mind gone? Those passages only served as an escape. For an emergency evacuation. This was a lone creature. It certainly didn't meet that level of desperation.

"Including the west side?"

"Yes."

"Perfect." Grinning widely, Thalasia refocused forward. A high-pitched musical note pierced the air. The cool breeze that once billowed through the tower, dancing with grains of sand, altered course. It picked up speed and churned a swirl of grit, like the onslaught of an oncoming storm no one could stop. "Let's go. Come on. Show me the way. No time to waste."

"What did you do?"

"A little redirection," she replied with a shrug, as if that answered it all.

Nurmoyes stared at her, but the female didn't budge. Whatever trick or action she'd taken, Thalasia kept it close at hand. Though they preferred otherwise, they didn't need to know. Their gaze flicked briefly to the guard. "It's changing course."

Not much, but it was better than what they had before. With a dip of their chin, Nurmoyes leaped from the tower and darted toward the central part of the village. They glanced back once, ensuring Thalasia trailed after them.

As they wound through the huts, they noted all the wood slates locked in place and tested the clean air with their antennae for any hint of aroma. Anything that could bring the mammolisk farther into their walls. Only the tangy scent of limestone tickled their antennae as they approached the hoodoos, rising like unsteady obelisks. Easing their descent, their feet touched the ground at the mouth of the darkened corridor leading out. "Here."

"Does it divert it at all?" Thalasia asked as she landed. "Or is it a straight shot?"

"There are multiple intersecting pathways; however, they all lead outside the village."

"Then you'll need to show me the way. The route that is the quickest, but will put us out,"—she paused and tilted her head—"the westernmost point."

Their eyebrows furrowed as the child gestured for them to lead the way. That made little sense. Even if the mammolisk came around in this direction, then she'd run right into it. "What do you hope to accomplish?"

"Well, given the ground that thing covered and how fast it moved, I'm banking that we're faster." A wide grin spread across her face. "Which would give us the element of surprise. Now, come on. That thing is tracking something mighty enticing. So, let's go."

Tracking? What had she done with that whistle? Nurmoyes had never once seen Adoni—or any of the golden sirens, for that matter—execute anything like it. "Which is what? Exactly?"

Thalasia started forward and spun around once as she uttered a single, terrifying word, "Me."

"What?" Nurmoyes snapped. This wasn't what they signed on for, nor expected. Of all the foolish things she could've done, it had to be that.

"I didn't stutter. It needed a tasty morsel to hunt, so I gave it one. See. Progress. Now, come on! We're wasting time. Something we don't have a lot of. Let's move."

"No," Nurmoyes declared. "We are not using you as bait." That wasn't how they functioned. It didn't matter whether they liked the teenager. Her life wasn't something to toy with.

"Too late. Now, let's go! Or I go on my own. And then you'd best pray I don't destroy your exit."

Shit. They had two options. Neither seemed like a good way to go, but the latter might end with the least amount of damage. Grumbling under their breath, Nurmoyes launched into the air and darted forward, flying around several bends, winding through the dark, damp underground corridor. *Luna, save me from this child.* Before she became the end of them.

The smooth stone brushed a few times across their antennae as they rounded the corner. Dirt from the ground peppered their feet. The nearer they drew to the exit, the drier the air became. Wind whistled just ahead. Moonlight shone down, highlighting the cracked clay beds where water once flowed. Slowing their flight, Nurmoyes eased on their approach.

A deep rumble bounced off the high canyon walls, spooking a nearby lizard, which quickly scampered through a patch of dead grass. Thalasia strode forward, stepping around them. *Damn it.* Nurmoyes reached for her, but she shrugged off their hold and tucked her wings back, emphasizing the jagged, discolored skin. What in the world? Scars? No, that couldn't be. Shoving their thoughts and questions aside, they trailed after Thalasia.

The growl grew louder. Heavy footsteps echoed, practically surrounding them. The corner of Thalasia's mouth twitched as a bright-white light sparked across the tips of her fingers. Moving close to a wall, she crouched down on her haunches. Although it all happened in a matter of seconds, it all seemed completely drawn out. Still, Nurmoyes would never forget what occurred next.

The mammolisk's massive head came around the corner. Large droplets of saliva spilled from its maw as it chuffed and sniffed the air, staring at the blue-winged siren with hunger. As it lunged, she shot into the air, pitching across the tunnel. The sole of her right foot hit the wall. Pushing off with great power, she swung a glaring-white bolt over her head and thrust it in a downward arc. It pierced the mammolisk's leathery hide. The creature's eyes bulged as gouts of blood gushed from its head, staining the earth crimson.

Nurmoyes blinked. Aside from the slight rise and fall of Thalasia's chest, the only thing they noticed was the faint thud as the beast's heavy body hit the ground. She'd done it. This child had actually killed a mammolisk. How? What weapon had she possessed? And where had it gone? Nurmoyes closed the short distance between the two of them, scouring Thalasia's hands, the dirt floor, even the creature. Nothing. Whatever she had used had completely disappeared.

Thalasia cracked a grin. "You can get rid of this, right? Otherwise, it might draw some unwanted attention. And we wouldn't want that."

"Um, yes." Or so they supposed. Burning it might have the same result, but they could figure it out. It wasn't the first time they had had to address an unusual situation.

"Good. Then I'm gonna head back while you stew on what just went down." The female spun on the back of her heel and started forward.

How had it all happened? How had she succeeded where others had failed? What powers did she possess? Was she truly what they needed? Despite all the questions running through their mind, nothing came out as they stared after her. Their gaze zeroed in on the markings that lanced her back. "Answer me one thing."

"What?"

"The scars. How did you—"

"No!" Thalasia declared, cutting them off as she faced them. "You don't get any part of my past. All you needed to know was that I can fight. And I've proven that."

That she had. In more ways than one. Maybe she was a child, but what burned behind those silver eyes was more than any child should experience. Najjar was right. Thalasia was special.

Nurmoyes blew out a soft breath. "You're right." They might prefer otherwise, but she didn't owe them an explanation any more than they owed her one. That might change, but for now, it seemed prudent to accept what was most important. She could help.

That gave them hope. With her, freedom might actually be attainable. That was something these people deserved.

Four

Thalasia struggled under the weight of the carcass. Just because she had control of her vocals and used that to direct wind currents didn't mean she could carry the dead mammolisk. Not that she had much farther to go. Whose brilliant idea was this again?

Yours, dumbass.

Right. Distraction 101, especially with a small village. This place had little in the way of entrance points and guards. From up here, she'd gather... maybe ten or more? Shit. They really should've thought this through better. Not that they'd had a lot of time to come up with a plan. Scanning the outskirts of the settlement, Thalasia noted the pattern of the two guards at the front gate, another eight monitoring the workers, and another six posted at various intervals along the inner wall.

Alright. Sixteen. All of them appeared more focused on keeping people in rather than on what might come from outside. She could handle this. It was all about... targeting. Locating the central-most barren spot, Thalasia took aim and released her load. "Bombs away," she muttered.

With the sun beating down on her back, she watched as the massive creature plummeted through the sky, eyeballing it like a hawk hunting its prey. Wind whipped around it, making no sound. Or so it seemed. No one immediately lifted his or her eyes and even looked toward the corpse. At least not until it hit the ground with a loud boom, like thunder echoing through the sky.

All eyes turned toward that large body. Now she just needed these fuckers to cluster. Then she could make it... well, rain. "Come on, come on, come on. Move. A little closer."

It had taken some work. This realm didn't exactly have fuel or black powder. However, it had a massive creature that expelled sulfur. And with a little finagling, she'd found an oxidizer and charcoal. All it needed now... the corner of her mouth lifted as a few guards closed in on the mangled remains, searching the sky. Not that they'd see her coming.

Thalasia charged a bolt and shot it straight at the beast. As the white heat connected with its target, igniting a collection of material, the dead mammolisk burst apart. The guards who had gathered flew across the village, slamming into various huts and parts of the wall. Chunks of flesh sailed through the air, landing all over. Workers screamed and scrambled, jerking on their chains.

That worked out better than she had hoped.

Summoning several more bolts, she dove toward the village just as Nurmoyes and their soldiers engaged the sentry at the front gate. She threw one bolt after another, striking down as many draconis as possible. Her dagger wouldn't get past their dragon-scales. Nor would the swords their army brandished. The lizards seemed like the bigger threat. So, she'd save her blade for any ape-like babians she crossed and use her powers on the lizards with dragon hides.

Landing right in the middle of it all, she didn't wait for an invitation to join in the fray. Thalasia withdrew her silver blade, lunged at the closest monkey-brain, and stabbed it in the shoulder. As she ripped the razor-sharp edge from its flesh, blood spurted everywhere. She ducked, dodging the scimitar that came swinging at her. Driving the tip of her dagger into a fur-covered chin, she hurled another silver bolt at the next opponent and fired several sharpened quills from her wings, striking her enemies in the arms, legs, and one between the eyes.

There was no telling how long the fight itself lasted. Nor did she track the number of lives she claimed. None of that mattered in the long run. Just the movement. Never stopping until it was finished. It was just like any other part of the dance her father had trained her to execute—attack, stab, duck, dodge, and strike. She kept up the rhythmic flow until they'd dispatched of every enemy.

When it finally reached its conclusion, Thalasia stared out at the carnage, her chest rising and falling with ragged breaths. Dismembered bodies lay strewn across the village. The ground was slick with the enemy's blood, pooling in a multitude of places. She hardly noticed the coppery stench as it wafted through the dust-choked air. Which seemed strange. Then again, maybe not. She hadn't become immune to it all. There were just too many scents to sort them all out.

Maybe she hadn't pushed for diplomacy as her parents had taught her. At least not here lately. Instead, she always went right into the battle. But you couldn't always avoid a fight. Especially not in this realm and not today. Not with freedom on the line.

Nurmoyes eyed Thalasia out of the corner of their eye as they unwound the link of chains shackled around the villager's wrists and ankles. Najjar, two soldiers, and the blue-winged teenager stacked the corpses and body parts together in a pile. After removing the restraints, the guardian dipped their chin at the female. "You're free now."

"Thank you! Oh, thank you."

They paid little mind as the woman darted off, joining a group of nearby villagers. Their gaze settled on Thalasia. While they had watched with more awe than expected as she'd fought earlier, it wasn't her movements that caught them off guard. She'd certainly dispelled any misgivings they had regarding her abilities last night. It was the aftermath. And her reaction. Or lack thereof.

She'd just stood there, blood spattered all over her person, sweat pouring down her face, surveying the land as if she hadn't just mutilated many draconis and babians. Her eyes had glazed over as if those creatures didn't exist. Like they were nothing more than bugs beneath her feet. Had she noticed any of them? Or what she'd accomplished?

Maybe they should've spoken with her more before going into battle alongside her. Learned more of her history. That could've better prepared them for what to expect. Though she'd readily refused to discuss it, they could've convinced her. Thalasia didn't appear… heartless or cold, but that response, it suggested otherwise.

Najjar strode across the clearing, sidling up next to them. "We're almost finished."

Their eyebrows drew together as they continued observing the way Thalasia carried herself. "How is she doing?" As much as they tried, they couldn't keep the concern out of their tone.

"Honestly?" the dark-haired female sighed. "Quiet. Focused. I can't determine much beyond that. Do you think there's something going on with her?"

"I'm uncertain." How else could they answer that? At least not without giving all of their thoughts away. There was still much to accomplish for the day. They just had to watch Thalasia closely. Any sign that something seemed off and they'd alter course.

Silver sparks rippled across the teenager's fingers. She flicked her wrist toward the pile of carcasses, igniting a fire. Flames licked at the flesh, fur, and scales. "We should get moving," Thalasia called out. "We don't want that to draw attention before we've started toward the next settlement."

Together, Nurmoyes and Najjar joined the female. "There is no rush. Besides, we should ensure our people are good and settled." The inhabitants here weren't fighters. It was how the village had become overrun with the enemy. They had to get their soldiers situated before moving on.

Thalasia faced them both. "That isn't exactly wise in war. Right now, we have the element of surprise working for us. Once they know of my presence, they'll heighten security and make it that much harder for us to take them out."

"Which will take time. No colony is close to any other. There is enough distance between here and Jandal that time is on our side. And if we leave these people ill-prepared, then our actions will be for naught."

"Nurmoyes is right, Thalasia. We need to do right by the townsfolk," Najjar said. "These are farmers and workers. Fighting isn't in their nature."

Rolling her silver eyes, the teenager scoffed. "Fine. One hour. Then we move on. In the meantime, I'll go fortify the gate and outer wall." Without another word, she stalked off.

Rubbing her thumb across her forehead, Najjar glanced at them as if they could explain what had just happened. "Am I missing something? Or did she completely shrug off our advice, like we don't have more experience than she does?"

"You are not wrong." Though they gathered she'd endured more than any child should ever suffer. It wasn't just in her words, or even her tone, but in how she acted. As if she knew how dark the world could truly be. That worried them. For reasons they dared not consider right then. "Nor is her concern misplaced."

"No, it isn't."

"An hour is sufficient time to get guards and precautions in place. Let us move." Because if things continued at this rate, it would make for an endless day. But they'd set hundreds free from the warlocks' reign, leading them closer to Adoni. That would make it all worthwhile.

Drach drummed his fingers against the ornate carvings of his throne's arm as he listened to his brother drone on and on regarding that damn siren. The male had nearly ruined everything yesterday, failing to execute a little fucking patience. They hadn't spent all these years stealing power from every golden siren for nothing.

"We must wait until her eighteenth year of birth when she is at full power," Nox objected. "There is no way around that."

"And if that ripple turns out to be something? Then what? Do you think the townsfolk will keep in line while we wait?"

As much as he loathed the idea of agreeing with Kaspar, the male had a point. To a degree. "Then that is our failing." And something they could address. His amber eyes swung toward the heavy, oak doors as they split wide. Something had happened. Or perhaps they'd finally obtained information regarding that disturbance.

A collector marched forward, approaching the dais at a clipped rate. The male's scaly head bowed as he dropped to a single knee in front of them. "My lords."

The stoic features of the draconis' face didn't bode well. Straightening against the throne's hard back, Drach reached to his left and stroked the dark, silken locks of his pet's head. "What news do you bring?"

"The humans have risen against your followers and reclaimed three of your colonies, my lords."

"What?" Kaspar slammed his fist down, nearly cracking the elaborate throne's armrest. The entire platform shook beneath them. "How is that possible?!"

"They had someone with mystical means fighting alongside them. Reports have provided little in the way of details. We know they have retaken Bardaris, Jandal, and Khobala. And the one assisting them… it is female."

Drach sat upright. The grip he had on the crown of his pet's head tightened. She whimpered. Not that he paid it much mind. "*Female?* Are you certain?"

The draconis leveled its beady eyes on him. "Yes, my lord."

Exchanging a glance with his brothers, he shook his head. "I know what you're thinking, and it's impossible." Female or not, there was no fucking way a witch had survived. They'd spent decades beheading those mystical beasts. It had taken them that long to fuck their way through the population, ensuring they located every woman earmarked with power. Whether a witch had tapped into her magic, a true sorceress bore a circular mark on the inside of her right thigh. Those creatures were the only ones who threatened their existence.

Nox's smooth brow wrinkled. "What else could it be?"

That was a damn good question. One he didn't have an answer for. But they'd come too far for anything to go wrong now. Though it seemed even more likely that Kaspar was right. They didn't have the time to wait for their golden siren to reach her full power. The corner of Kaspar's mouth twitched. Not that his brother uttered a word. Nor was it necessary. Drach cursed under his breath and glared at their subordinate. "Take four other collectors with you. *Find* me some answers. Do you understand, Lapa?"

"Yes, my lord." With a low dip of his chin, he rose to his feet. The doors clapped shut behind him as he exited the throne room.

For the first time in centuries, the rich color of the draperies matched how he felt. Not that he'd allow it to consume him. He hadn't fought all this time and come this far just to walk away now. Even if it meant he had to get his hands a little dirty.

A maniacal grin spread across Kaspar's face as he steepled his fingers, leaning back in his chair. "A little interrogation could work wonders, brother."

"I know," Drach hissed. He didn't need confirmation. Nor the suggestion. Had the male forgotten all he'd done to get them here? Of course not. His brother simply wanted an excuse to play. Not happening. "I stand by what I said. You stay away from her, Kaspar. Understood?" He stood. "Nox and I will handle it."

"That's fine." Kaspar smirked. "I'm always a summon away. Until then, I think I'll keep your pet company."

Drach shot across the room, grabbed his brother by the throat, and slammed him into the wall behind their thrones. "Touch one hair on her head and it'll be the last thing you do. Got it?"

"Got it," the male squeaked.

"Drach!" Nox hollered, yanking at his arm. "Let him go!"

Ensuring his brother fully understood the extent of his threat, he tightened the hold he had, cutting off more of the male's air supply. When those amber eyes flared, Drach released Kaspar and let him crumple to the floor. Not that the carpet offered much cushion. That just seemed to emphasize his message more, especially as his brother coughed, struggling to gather oxygen into his lungs. Good. The male deserved it.

Drach glanced at Nox. "Let's go." He spun on his heel and stalked toward the exit. They had work to do.

"I don't know!" Adoni screamed. How many times could she give them the same answer before they accepted it as truth? Even their questions had become repetitive. Did they think it would alter the outcome? The rough palm of the male's hand connected with her cheek. Her toes scraped the dirt floor as he struck her for the tenth time.

"Tell me who she is!"

"I told you." Her right eye had already swollen shut. Her tongue snaked out across her bloody lip. She grimaced at the slight sting. At least it took away from the throbbing in her face and the burning sensation around her wrists. She'd almost take the chains over the ropes they'd bound and strung her up with. Almost like she was a pig up for slaughter. "I don't know."

"You have been in *that* wasteland your entire life. I. Don't. Believe. You," he snarled.

What more did the warlock think he could do to her? Though her vision swam in crimson and her world tilted with a throbbing ache, an icy dread sharpened her senses. He needed her. Alive! Yeah, he'd make it hurt, but he wouldn't kill her. Not yet.

"Drach, she may know nothing."

"She must!" The male roughly dragged a hand through his long, gray hair, knotting the strands up in his fingers. His gaze narrowed. "What do we know of her guardian? Was it killed when the hunter collected her?"

"No. According to reports, it wasn't present. So, it may already be dead."

Surely they wouldn't send a hunter or collector back after Nurmoyes? Not if she kept her trap shut. If these warlocks didn't know her guardian still lived, then they had nothing to hold over her. She'd stick with the same answer. No matter what they asked.

The younger of them peered at her. Drawing to his full height, he closed the distance between them. He squinted, focusing his amber gaze on her. The faintest hint of a smirk settled at the corner of his mouth as he jutted his chin. "Hmm. You must think you hold all the power because we need you alive. However, that's inaccurate." Turning slightly toward his companion, he pointed a finger at her. "This isn't getting us anywhere, but a reminder that there is a price for her failure to respond should do the trick. While I get her cleaned up, go into the city and select three young maidens."

"Yes, of course." Drach clapped his hands together. "A public display... that should certainly loosen her tongue."

Maidens? No, they wouldn't hurt young girls just to punish her. Would they? They'd kidnapped her. Taken all the other golden sirens, killed every last one, and their guardians, enslaved humans, and more. Torturing a few young girls to punish her was just another part of their script. Adoni shook her head. "No... please... I'll tell you whatever you want! Just don't hurt them." What else could she do? Enough people had suffered at their hands. Even if she knew nothing, she'd come up with something.

"I don't believe you," the younger warlock stated. "Anything that you say now is tainted. You had your opportunity. Now, you'll see what happens when you fail to provide answers."

Drach sneered. "I couldn't agree more." His gaze flicked to the other male. "Enjoy your cleanup. I'll be ready by the time you're finished." He spun around on his heel and marched out of the dungeon, the thick door clinking shut behind him.

The junior warlock stepped behind her and tightened the bindings holding her wings down. She groaned as the leather bit into her flesh. There had to be something she could do. Something she hadn't thought of. A way to stop this from happening. She didn't want anyone to die on her behalf. Her gaze bounced between the walls and the iron bars. Even if she could escape right then, she wouldn't get far. "Please," Adoni pled. "I'll tell you whatever you want to know. Just don't hurt them."

Stepping in front of her, the male smirked. "I don't think you understand there are repercussions for your actions. This is one of them. Now, don't move. This might hurt a little. And a public display will matter little if you aren't there to bear witness." His hand hovered in front of her face. A bright white, feverish light shone from his palm.

At first, it only stung as the damage to her cheek became undone, slowly knitting itself back together. The pain quickly transitioned into something more as it went deeper, burrowing beneath her skin. Past the muscle. Down to the bone. It felt like she was being hollowed out and stuffed. She screamed at the agony penetrating every inch of her body. Not that she could say how long it lasted. Just that at some point, it became too much. As she sagged against her restraints, darkness claimed her, and the world around her faded into nothingness.

Five

Thalasia stared out across the sand and rocky landscape. While she appreciated the background noise of celebratory joy, she preferred to focus on guard duty. They'd accomplished a lot today, but not enough to her liking. Although they'd freed a few villages, giving the slaves their lives back, they'd also depleted some of their numbers, which they had had little to start with. With every settlement they regained, some of their soldiers stayed behind. It was necessary.

Even if they weren't done.

The cold air ruffled her feathers. Tearing her gaze from the sea of vast canyons and crackled dry beds, she peered over her shoulder at the party. The central clearing teemed with life, the community dancing around the rising flames. It was a sight to see them all raise their voices, reveling in their success. Maybe this was part of her purpose. Not just rescuing the golden siren, but giving all of them hope.

As the festivities continued, Thalasia turned her attention back to guard duty, focusing on the terrain beneath the moonlight. What the hell was that? Her gaze narrowed at the sight ahead. Dust kicked up against the velvety-black night sky. Something was running in their direction, but from this distance, she couldn't quite make out what. Maybe it wasn't anything to worry about. There were a lot of creatures that hunted during the night. Many of which had nothing to do with the warlocks or their minions.

This was likely no different.

Still, it was best to monitor it closely. Leaning on the wooden banister, Thalasia stared at the animal until she identified it. *A wild dog.* She'd never seen one up close, but they appeared in a few realms in her journal. Especially the human ones. Definitely not something for her to fret over. Except it barreled right for the village, kicking up dirt and grime in its wake. Slowly, she drew to her full height of five-eight. That wasn't normal. "I'll be right back," she muttered as she launched into the air and took to the sky. There was no reason to say anything else to the actual guard until she knew more.

Her wings flapped as she flew against the wind. Thalasia tilted her head down, dropping her gaze to everything below. Given how quickly she'd taken off, it was the only option to keep the grit out of her eyes. Not that she could see anything from this height beyond the displaced sand. Shit. The dog was running too fast. She had to get closer. It was the only way she could make a full assessment.

Turning back toward the village, Thalasia scanned the surface and quickly located a spot amidst the wind-worn rock formations where she could land. From there, she could cut the animal off, maybe even deter its approach. It wasn't much of a solution, but better than nothing, considering the murky situation. If she were lucky, this would all be for nothing. Though that rarely seemed to be the case.

Thalasia dove toward the towering, layered rock walls. She slowed down, landing softly on the cool sand. As she faced the dunes and beyond, the wind whipped around the loose strands of her blue hair. Great. Just something else she needed to struggle against.

The creature closed in fast, approaching the village's front gates. No, she couldn't let this happen. Without a second thought, Thalasia summoned a bolt of lightning, striking down close to the creature. Not that it deterred it. Instead, it just veered around the fulgurite and kept right on running. *Shit.* Wasn't it a normal animal? Could it possibly be something they hadn't told her about? Refusing to give up, Thalasia palmed a bolt and charged toward the creature.

The dog growled low and met her head-on.

Or attempted to.

Nurmoyes came down directly between them. "Stop!"

"What are you doing?" Thalasia hollered as she skidded to a stop, nearly plowing right into the guardian.

Nurmoyes' pale eyes shifted from her to the wild dog, who had also halted. "What are you doing here, Arietta?"

Arietta? That thing had a name? What the fuck was going on here? Who the hell was this? Why hadn't Nurmoyes told her anything about—*Holy shit!* Her eyes widened as the bolt disintegrated in her hand.

Bones snapped and cracked as the animal transformed into a female with long, jet-black hair hanging down her back. The woman stood a little shorter than her. A plum-colored gaze sized her up. "Is she the one?"

'The one' what? Why were they talking about her as if she wasn't standing right there in front of them? What the fuck? Thalasia opened her mouth—Nurmoyes cut her off.

"Yes, but you didn't answer the question. Why are you here?"

"We needed to make you aware of what transpired earlier and I volunteered for the trip."

"'We?' We who?" Thalasia snapped. Cocking her hip out, she folded her arms across her chest and glared at the two of them. One of them needed to explain what the fuck they were going on about. Because it somehow seemed to involve her.

Nurmoyes let out a long, drawn-out sigh and gestured toward the gates. "Perhaps it is best if we discuss this inside."

"Then lead the way." She hadn't helped them reclaim three communities just to be left at the wayside. Her mission was far from over. She wouldn't succeed if they didn't give her every bit of viable information. That couldn't happen.

Failure wasn't an option.

Nurmoyes eyed the council members as their collective voices rose over one another. The news that Arietta had shared had put them in a precarious position. None of them could agree on what their next steps should encompass. That was only one of their major problems. Thalasia's reaction to everything was the other.

"You've had witches at your disposal this whole time and you didn't think I should be made aware of this?!"

"It isn't that simple." Nurmoyes pinched the bridge of their nose. *"The 'Sisters of Serenity' are protected. The warlocks tried to wipe them completely out. Without this coven, we have no hope of ever overcoming the damage to our society."*

"What do you think is happening now? Your resistance hadn't exactly accomplished anything before I arrived." Groaning, Thalasia threw her hands up in the air and shook her head. She blew out a heavy breath. *"And the warlocks know now, which was bound to happen. So, does this mean you stop? Lose what little momentum we gained today? Or are you continuing forward?"*

"That is going to be for the council to decide. We have to consider this news."

Her silver gaze narrowed as she folded her arms across her chest. "You had to expect them to retaliate when the news of our actions reached them. Why do you think I pushed you for us to move as fast as we could? To save as many as possible? Once they knew of our movement, they have both the chance to react and gather their forces. The warlocks will try to stop us."

"I stand by the choice we made. If we'd left those encampments without reinforcements, then what we've done would make no difference. We would be lucky if anything remained."

"Nurmoyes!" Najjar snapped.

"Yes?" They blinked as the entire council stared blankly at them. Whatever the group had decided, they'd completely missed it.

"So, you're certain Arietta's information is true and factual?"

Crap. Were they back on that again? Each council member sat there in utter silence, as if impatiently awaiting their response. Nurmoyes's lips pinched together as they drummed their fingers against the large, rounded, wooden table. This was completely ridiculous. How many times did they have to cover this? "Yes. The warlocks publicly whipped three young girls, stripped them naked, and hung them, claiming it as a punishment for our actions. They told those gathered, if no one came forth regarding those included in the... Opposition," they got the single word out through gritted teeth, "then their punishments will continue." Everything about the claim was an assault on the people. They weren't the *opposition*. That title belonged to the warlocks and those who blindly followed them. Their lives were better before those monsters took over. For the love of Luna. Was the blue-haired siren right?

Thalasia had gotten annoyed with them, thrown her hands in the air and stormed off, making one last comment. As the council once again started screaming over one another, they replayed her words in their mind. This was truly getting them nowhere. Some members pointed out the lives that the warlocks might claim, while others believed it was worth the risk. It was the same crap that the council had spewed over the last hour. They couldn't take it anymore. Nurmoyes slammed their fist down on the table. The thing shook underneath the strike. "Enough!"

Everyone stopped talking. The entire room went silent. Nurmoyes jabbed a finger at each of them. "For years, we have done the same thing over and over. Where has that gotten us? Until today, nowhere. Countless lives lost. Golden sirens gone. Guardians gone. Humans enslaved. How much blood must we give?" Leaning back, they ensured they had every-one's full attention before they continued. This was far too important. "We cannot keep repeating the same steps and expect a different outcome. We have two options. One, we gather those we've saved here at the sanc-tuary city, fortify our home, and prepare to fight. The warlocks know where we are. They proved that when they kidnapped Adoni yesterday. Or two, we call their bluff and keep moving forward. We know what they have stated publicly, but we don't know what they've stated behind closed doors. Even with the coven on our side, that knowledge isn't available to us. Yes, it is a risk, but either way, we're going to war. The question is, are we letting them bring it to us or are we taking it to them?" They paused, letting the weight of their words sink in. "What say you?"

Thalasia tried to stand, but the cold, heavy chains held her firmly in place. She couldn't even determine the time of day. Only one way existed for her to track the passage of time—a mark on the wood of the wall with charcoal she'd found on the floor. It wasn't much, but it helped. Not that anyone searched for her. Both of her parents had died. Why did it matter how much time had gone by? What was the point in knowing how long these psychopaths had kept her trapped down here in this dank dungeon?

It was the only word she could think of to describe them. The dominant female—she didn't know her name. They all called her 'Mistress.' It was obvious that she was in charge. It was the same woman who'd instructed for her to be taken. How long ago was that? Her gaze drifted to the number of slashes on the wall. Thirty? Had she really been here for a month?

Or was that just the number of times they'd tortured her for information? For her visions. Or her ability to jump between realms. Gods, she didn't know anymore. Her body sagged against the heavy manacles. She whimpered as agonizing pain lanced through her back. It still burned from when they'd beaten her two days earlier. They hadn't just bound her wrists and ankles, but her wings, too. All so she couldn't use her power or go anywhere. Not that she hadn't tried. Each time she tried to escape, she'd failed. Once, she nearly lost her tongue. She hadn't attempted her siren song since.

Mistress caused her pain, yet saved her tongue. Not that it had been without purpose. Leaning her head against the rough texture of the wall, Thalasia sighed, a puff of air escaping her lips. She was weary, her eyelids heavy with exhaustion. But death wasn't even knocking on her door. Let alone in the vicinity.

The door to the cabin swung open with a whoosh of displaced air. Mistress entered the room. "Have you reconsidered yet?"

"Screw you." The woman wanted to know only one thing. It didn't matter that she had no comprehension of the mechanics. She refused to tell Mistress how to leave this realm.

"I will get what I want from you one way or another."

Thalasia laughed. She shouldn't have. It only pissed Mistress off more, but she couldn't stop it. No matter how many ways the woman tortured her—broken fingers, always snapped back into place to prevent shock; lashings, beatings; the one time she tried to have her raped and failed, thank the gods for small favors; or the pieces of skin removed—nothing had ever forced her to reveal that information. It had loosened her tongue with her visions, but nothing else. Even that had taken time. She'd held out for weeks before she caved. At least if her markings were accurate.

"Perhaps it is time we tried something new, then." Mistress narrowed her dark-gray eyes, glinting like storm clouds, and lifted her hand in the air, a silent signal.

Without being touched, Thalasia's body rose off the ground, her feet dangling ever so slightly. The chains limited her movement. Something tightened around her neck, obstructing her airway. Fuck! Her lungs burned, and she coughed, clawing at the invisible force that felt like suffocating smoke. Before she blacked out, the constriction on her lungs disappeared and she collapsed to the floor. Clutching her throat, Thalasia coughed repeatedly. It felt like she'd just tried to swallow a fire-poker.

"Are you ready to speak now?"

Struggling to catch her breath, a wave of dizziness washed over her as she tried to sit up for the third time. Thalasia fixed a furious glare on the female, her face contorted in a silent rage. "Go. To. Hell."

"Pity." The woman stepped away from the door and hopped up on a nearby table. "Bring them in."

Bring what in? The door opened again. First, a man with the same gray eyes as Mistress joined them. He had an older woman with graying hair slung over his shoulder. The male chained her to the other wall. Another woman, again with the same eyes as Mistress, followed right behind him. Except she had a little girl tossed over her shoulder. They'd strung up the blonde-headed little girl, and recognition set in place. They were from her latest vision—the one Mistress had pried out of her. Thalasia's eyes widened. This couldn't be happening. It was her job to save these people, not to bring them harm. Not cause their death.

"Tell me what I wish to know or sit there and watch them die. The choice is yours."

Her silver gaze snapped to Mistress, who'd closed the distance between them. When the fuck had that happened? Tears welled in the corners of her eyes. Shit. She couldn't choose. Neither was a good option. If she told Mistress the truth, would the female just kill all three of them? There had to be a way out of this. The door was still—Thalasia zeroed in on that heavy, iron door. She swallowed. They'd shut it. What was she supposed to do now? Where were the gods when she needed help?

Both the older woman and the little girl stirred.

"I will not ask you again. Make your choice."

Thalasia glanced back and forth between the prisoners and Mistress. What could she do? There wasn't a way out for any of them. It didn't matter what decision she made. That evil woman had no heart. Mistress cared about no one except herself. Whether she told her the truth or said nothing, the female would kill them. Thalasia shook her head, tears streaming silently down her face as she yanked with all her might on the chains that bit into her wrists. "No! I won't choose! You heartless bitch! I won't choose!"

"So be it." Mistress dipped her chin toward the two who looked like her as she draped one long leg over the other and leaned back as if she was settling in for a show.

"No!" Thalasia screamed, bolting upright. Her heart thundered behind her ribcage. Drawing her legs to her chest, she swept a shaky hand across her forehead, clearing away the beads of sweat. Shit. Where the fuck was she? Her gaze dropped to the heavy blanket covering her lower body. She spotted the metallic bar holding the cot in place.

Right. Village. The hut they'd given her for rest. Hanging her head, she heaved a deep breath. Her heart still felt like it might burst out of her chest. Though it seemed to calm down. Gods, she hated when *that* woman invaded her nightmares.

"Thalasia?"

Scrambling backward, she nearly fell out of the cot as her silver eyes snapped toward the voice. Her hand shot to her breastbone as heart raced. Her gaze narrowed. Someone took a step forward. The moonlight shone down, highlighting their sea-foam-green skin. *Motherfucker.* "What the fuck, Nurmoyes?" Seriously. Was nowhere sacred around here? "Are you trying to give me a heart attack?"

"Of course not. I would not wish any harm to you. However, you sounded in distress, so I thought I would check on you."

Yeah, Mistress had a way of doing that shit to her. Which meant she'd probably tossed and turned. Thalasia dragged a hand across the top of her sweat-drenched head. Fuck, It had been a bad one. "Well, as you can see, I'm fine."

"That does not appear to be the case." The guardian's antennae curled ever so slightly. "What happened, Thalasia? Where did you go in your mind?"

That wasn't fucking happening. "My past is off-limits." Hadn't she made that abundantly clear already? They didn't have a right to that information. Not that she probably should've even said that much. Though they were smart enough to figure it out on their own. Fuck. She just needed to change the subject. Something she could do easily. Since she was already awake. "Did the council come to a decision?"

Clasping their hands behind their back, Nurmoyes dipped their chin. "They have agreed it is imperative we move forward as originally planned."

"Good." For a moment, she'd worried their successes today wouldn't be enough, considering what the warlocks had done to those girls. Yeah, those fuckers reminded her way too much of Mistress. A female who still lived. That wouldn't happen here. Her gaze leveled on Nurmoyes and the way concern contorted their features. Nope. Definitely wouldn't happen here. "You should, uh, let me get back to sleep. We've got a long day tomorrow."

The guardian opened their mouth, snapped it shut, and nodded their head. "Yes, of course." They strode forward, heading toward the exit.

Stretching her legs out, Thalasia readjusted in the cot and tried to get comfortable. There was no telling whether it would happen. Sometimes after a nightmare like that, sleep eluded her. Other times, the dark abyss dragged her down without resistance.

"You may always speak to me," Nurmoyes called out. "Should you so choose."

They might as well forget that shit. "It'll never happen." The more she talked about it, the more power she gave it. And she'd given that bitch enough of that to last a fucking lifetime.

No one except the gods would ever have power over her ever again.

No. One.

Thalasia kicked the babian square in the chest, forcing it to stumble backward. It screeched as it lunged toward her. Dropping low, she swept her leg out and caught it right behind the ankle, knocking it off its feet. Without giving the creature a chance to get back up, she impaled it, driving her dagger into its heart. There wasn't time to waste on ensuring the babian stopped breathing. As long as it wasn't moving, the creature was dead. It was among the dozens of hunters they'd crossed in this town. Yanking her blade from the babian's body, she turned toward the battle.

A cacophony of triumphant war cries rang out, surrounding her from every direction.

Lowering her dagger to her side, Thalasia surveyed the remnants of the battlefield. The babians and draconis lay still, their blood seeping into the soil like tears staining a somber canvas. The sun glinted off the lively embers, painting the scene with the excitement of a new beginning, the remaining flames eager to rebuild. Her breath hitched, and a shiver ran down her spine as the acrid scent of burning flesh assaulted her nostrils. She swallowed, the bitter tang a reminder of the fight she had endured. Despite the gruesome scene that unfolded before her, the soldiers deserved a moment of celebration.

They'd reclaimed another town.

Only one remained before they turned their attention to the cityscape. Their goal was nearly within reach. Which meant her time here was almost at its end. Her vision blurred. *No!* Dear gods, no. This wasn't happening now. Maybe she could hold it back. Everything cleared, but not for more than a few seconds. A cold sweat slicked her palms as her heartbeat hammered against her ribs, each breath a shallow gasp.

"No," Thalasia mumbled. All of her senses awakened, heightening until she heard and saw every little detail that surrounded her. Minor sounds reverberated as if they were right in her ears. Blood from the tip of her blade hit the ground with a faint *drip, drip.* The sun's rays bounced off the crimson puddle mere inches from her foot, almost making it appear black. A fly landed on a nearby broken shaft. It buzzed, buzzed through the air. The hold she had around the dagger's hilt loosened. Fuck. This was happening, whether or not she wanted it.

Her eyes rolled back in her head. Thalasia stumbled backward, barely making it to a tall, wooden post before her legs gave out underneath her. The last thing she heard as she went down was someone calling out her name.

"You don't seem to know much of anything, do you?" Glowering at the young female dangling in front of him, he tightened the hold he had on her jaw. "No smart-ass comments this time?"

"Drach, that's enough. If you keep this up, we'll have to heal her again. It's best that we don't waste the power."

"Right," he smirked. "Or the time. She'll be dead soon enough."

Despite the manacles locked around her wrists and the chains wrapped around her wings, the young female laughed as if the threat didn't bother her. "No matter what you do, you know it won't be enough. Which means you'll fail and have killed me for nothing. All because you couldn't wait."

With a scoff, Drach jutted his chin. "That's what you think." A malicious grin slowly crossed his dark features, twisting his face into a mask of cruel amusement. "We figured out how to draw your magic forth. All. Of. It."

"Our hunters should be out retrieving everything we need now," the other male added.

Her brown eyes widened, reflecting the fear that washed over her as her face paled. "No!" She jerked against the chains, the clinking of metal echoing in the silence as she fought for her freedom.

"Oh, yes." A harsh bark erupted from his throat. "Your little blue-haired friend and your guardian will be in our hands soon."

Thalasia groaned as the sun glared angrily into her eyes. Shit. She hated when a vision came on like that. She blinked at the muffled sound of someone's voice. It sounded so far off. Was she on her back? That didn't seem right. She could've sworn she'd face-planted it before her world went all tilt-a-whirl. Or maybe she'd just imagined that. Stuff like that happened with her visions. Yep. For the glimmer of what might be, she surrendered her peace, a dull ache settling deep within her skull, and a chilling premonition of aches that would shadow her steps. Slowly, the cold and rough stone walls of the dank dungeon disappeared. A pair of slender, fuzzy antennae and a set of pale eyes replaced it. "Nurmoyes?" she choked out.

"Thank Luna. Are you alright?" the guardian prodded. "You went down, and no one could get through to you."

Oh, how to answer that? The scorching heat intensified the throbbing in her head, a relentless, pounding ache. Fuck. That was highly uncomfortable. If she sat up... oh, look, she was lying down. Thalasia moaned, easing into a sitting position as she pressed the heel of her palm against the cool earth. It didn't totally extinguish the sharp stabs in her gray matter, but it helped. "Yeah," she mumbled. "I'm all right. Just... uh... a little gift from the gods." Yeah, those fuckers had a twisted sense of humor at her expense.

Nurmoyes sat back on the soles of their feet as their eyebrows furrowed. "Meaning?"

Yeah, she refused to elaborate on even the smallest detail. That revelation always opened the floodgates and brought on far too many insistent questions. Instead, she mentally replayed the scene, lingering on every detail, and chose the simplest explanation. Because that was the bottom line. "That we're running out of time."

"Care to clarify?"

Nope. Not at all. Thalasia just stared at the guardian. "It requires not more clarification than that." Nurmoyes didn't need to know what she'd seen. They were already moving as fast as they could. Any faster would cause mistakes. Deadly ones.

Though if her vision was anything to go by, they were on track for that, anyway. No reason to point out the obvious. Or add to their current stress. They knew what they had to do.

Fight.

"You see it, don't you?" Najjar asked.

The female had a way with the questions tonight. How long had they discussed this now? Though she certainly had a point. The same one she'd made two nights ago. As the flames danced, casting a warm glow on their face against the night sky, Nurmoyes crossed one ankle over the other and thought back to their conversation with Thalasia.

"You've seen something, haven't you?" There wasn't much to suggest that was true, except for Thalasia's refusal to give a direct response. Nothing on the teenager's face gave anything away. While they could use their powers and learn what they wished, they preferred not to.

"How did you…?" Her words trailed off. An incredulous look crossed Thalasia's features. "I didn't think you believed me."

"Truly?" Nurmoyes frowned, their lips pressed into a thin, displeased line. When had they given her that impression? From the beginning, they'd believed her words. Not that they'd given her any choice but to tell the truth. Something she may not yet be aware of. "I know the gods have a tendency to… as you so eloquently put it, gift, certain abilities to those of their choosing. Just because you have foreseen it does not mean it will come to pass."

Thalasia smirked, a silent challenge in the curve of her mouth. "That's why they send me to these places. To stop whatever it is I've seen. It's also why I can tell you that we're running out of time. The warlocks figured out how to draw her powers out. All of them."

"What?" they asked as a faint smirk settled on Najjar's face.

"I can see a storm brewing in that head of yours. Like maybe it's all finally coming together?"

"Yes, I have seen Thalasia's value." That wasn't the problem. At least not anymore. It was what they hadn't gotten out of the female. Nor did they believe they could. The teenager seemed rather disinclined to share any part of her past. Something they believed could benefit her. Even Adoni. And what they hadn't decided regarding their charge. Truthfully, they hadn't protected her. Not as well as they should have. Taking her from town to town had been a poor decision on their part. Getting Adoni away from the warlocks was only half the solution.

"But you don't know what to do with that, do you?"

"Not entirely." Nurmoyes rubbed their face raw, a desperate attempt to ground themselves in the overwhelming chaos. How did they explain their perspective without Najjar going into another rant? No matter what they offered, that seemed highly unlikely. The female's unsolicited advice was rarely wrong. Maybe she'd have something now that could help, even if it included a lengthy response. "Thalasia doesn't seem to trust anyone. Given the way she lives, I cannot fault her for that. Though knowing more would aid in what comes once we rescue Adoni."

"Have you considered that you're going about this all wrong?"

"Meaning?" It wasn't as if they hadn't attempted a variety of questions. They'd done that, utilizing their extensive knowledge without their abilities. Nothing had worked.

"You've been going at her directly. Perhaps if you take a more... indirect approach,"—Najjar dipped her chin, gesturing toward her son. "Then you might succeed."

Get the information they sought through a third party. Hmm. It seemed possible. Unless, of course, Urbi refused to share what he discovered afterward. At this rate, what could it hurt? They'd tried everything else, to no avail. They had few options left. "Perhaps."

"I'm just saying Urbi is closer to her age. He might have luck."

"And if that does not work?" Because they had to consider it might fail as all the others had.

Najjar tilted her head. "Well, then it leaves you with only one other choice. And you don't need me to tell what *that* is. Do you?"

"No," Nurmoyes muttered. They didn't. Because if Urbi failed, then all that remained was a trade. Information for information. They'd limited what got shared with the blue-siren. It was all they could do to protect Adoni. If that meant one last attempt using anything but that, then so be it.

It mattered little that it was doomed to fail.

They couldn't risk laying all their cards out. Not yet.

Urbi climbed the last rung of the ladder, peering around the wooden box that comprised the watchtower. The gritty wind whipped around Thalasia as she leaned against the corner post, arms folded across her chest, staring out across the endless sea of dunes, fully prepared for any form of attack. Or so it appeared. Clearing his throat, he drew those silver eyes in his direction as he pulled himself onto the platform. "I thought you could use some company."

"Really?" She cocked an eyebrow at him and shrugged her shoulders. "You're welcome to join me... I guess. It's kind of boring, though."

"That's okay. Boring can be nice sometimes." Besides, he'd come up with a purpose. A reason he didn't disclose to Thalasia. While Nurmoyes had asked him to learn about her, he wanted to do that on his own. For his own reasons. And if he didn't pepper her with questions right away, then he believed he'd get what he desired—to know her. That was exactly why Urbi had agreed to do this, but hadn't promised to share whatever he discovered with Nurmoyes. Something the guardian would survive.

"That depends on what you're used to."

He strolled over to where she lingered and leaned against the railing beside her. "What do you mean?"

"If you're accustomed to a lot going on, then the quiet only happens right before the storm. And typically means something bad is coming your way. Boring isn't good then. But if life is slow and you just kind of leisure your way through it, then... it's just normal."

That made sense. In a strange sort of roundabout way. Not that he'd ever heard it described like that. Then again, their lives generally weren't boring.

Not that he knew if that applied to her as well. "Do you think after what we accomplished today, this is just the quiet before the storm?"

"It's highly likely. We didn't back down. Instead, we reclaimed two more towns. I don't think the warlocks will care for that."

"Do you think they'll..." His words trailed off. Urbi shaking hand pressed against his neck, desperately trying to contain the rising hysteria. He needed her thoughts, but even to consider it felt like a desperate plea thrown into an uncaring universe. What if traveled through the air to the warlocks? Or one of their hunters or collectors?

"No," Thalasia replied, as if she'd figured out what he hadn't proposed. "They won't come at us the same way twice. Not after we called their bluff. They'll try something else. That's what worries me."

"Is that why you're up here watching the horizon instead of joining everyone else in the celebration?"

"Sort of."

Talk about a vague answer. That's what she'd given him. What was it supposed to mean? Urbi cocked an eyebrow at her. "'Sort of?'"

Crossing over to the other side of the box, Thalasia leaned forward against the railing. "I've traveled to so many realms that I've lost count. While I'm happy that the others can celebrate... my experience has taught me it's best not to do so too early. You never know what horrors the next day or night might bring."

That didn't help much. Did it mean she had no joy in her life? Or that she found it difficult to see amidst the darkness? "Is that what you think? That we've begun the festivities although we haven't yet won the war?"

Her silver stare swung back in his direction. "Yes. No." She blew out a heavy breath, a small cloud forming in the cold air. "I haven't exactly had things worth being joyful about. So, I tend to see the abyss and not the light."

That was it. Thalasia had suffered a lot. He didn't need the details; her gaze, once bright, now held only a vacant, muted grief that suffocated him. "You know that good can still happen amidst the bad, right?"

"Got any examples? Because I'm not sure I even know what it's like."

"Well... Adoni getting kidnapped is bad. Same with the collectors finding us." The corner of his mouth lifted. "But then Nurmoyes showed up with you. That seems like a good thing to me. I mean..." Urbi pushed off the railing and gestured to the ongoing noises below them. "Just look at what's happened because of you. For the first time in a long time, we're fighting back. We are hopeful that tomorrow will be a good day. That we will actually be free."

"Don't attribute all of that to me. I'm just here, doing what the gods sent me to do, and helping to the best of my abilities. The rest... that's the soldiers who have fought the battles. They deserve your gratitude."

"You don't take compliments very well, do you?" He'd given her a damn good one, too. Though he supposed they were both right. Thalasia was just one cog in the machine. Not the whole machine. Still, the council had kept to one response for years. Hide and run. It wasn't until she popped into the picture that they changed their tune. Or considered another direction.

"I'm not used to them." Thalasia's gaze dropped to the wooden floorboards as she kicked at the platform with the toe of her leather boot. A pained expression darkened her features as she rubbed at her chest, her knuckles white against her skin. "I don't... make friends... wherever I go. Life has... taken a lot from me." Her shoulders slumped, a faint tremble in her lip hinting at unspoken sorrow. "Seems smart not to get attached to those I'm around. Just do my job and leave. You know?"

Dear gods. An icy dread washed over Urbi as her words echoed in his mind, his mouth dry as dust. He really didn't want to ask, but he had to know. "You lost someone. Someone important." Though he tried, the words came out as a declaration, not a question. He shook his head as her eyes snapped in his direction, and he held up his hands in surrender. "I'm sorry. I shouldn't have said anything. You don't... you don't have to tell me." He rubbed his neck, a dull ache echoing the sorrow reflected in her eyes. Shit. Maybe he should just go.

Leaning in the railing, her hands met listlessly, fingers intertwined as if to contain her grief. Her eyes drifted from him, a distant mist settling with them. She peered out across the inky, star-dusted night sky.

"I'm just—"

"My parents. They risked their lives to save mine. Same with my guardian. I'm the last of my kind. That's why..." Thalasia paused. "It's why I don't befriend people."

That explained a lot. More than he had expected. "I'm sorry for your loss, Thalasia." He meant that, but gods, words didn't seem to go far enough to express how deep his sorrow for her went. Urbi strode across, stopping next to her, and leaned on the tower's framework with his elbows.

He drank in the various hues of the dark indigos and royal blues of the haze before him, his eyes drawn to the soft glow of the twinkling stars. "I know how it feels to lose a loved one. My father was killed in the raids before we moved here."

"I'm sorry to hear that." Slowly, she turned and took up a spot beside him, a few feet between them. "No one should know what that's like. Words never do the experience justice."

"No, they don't." He wouldn't wish it on anyone. Not even his worst enemy. Though he didn't think the warlocks felt much in that regard. "Things weren't always like this," he started.

"How so?"

The welcome distraction had come out of nowhere. It was something they both needed. Their conversation had taken a direction he was ill-prepared for. He hated talking about his father as much as it seemed she despised speaking of her parents. "From my understanding, when the golden sirens first arrived, we all welcomed them with open arms. We all lived together in harmony. Babians, draconis, mutuphin, sirens, warlocks, witches, humans... all of us."

"What changed?"

"This was all before my time, but my mother told me that the warlocks became overly ambitious. There weren't many of them in the beginning. I'm not entirely sure what happened. Just that they slowly grew in number and power. Though it never seemed enough. Then, about a hundred years ago, something shifted. No one really knows what. Just that over time, warlocks and witches died... nearly into extinction. The same with the mutuphin and sirens. Nurmoyes and Adoni are all that remain." He might've over-explained it all, but that was how he'd learned it. Minus a lot of details that he'd left out. The specifics mattered little in the end.

Her brows pinched together as she stared at him in confusion. "I thought Nurmoyes was Adoni's guardian."

"That's right." Urbi cracked a grin. "Nurmoyes's species is mutuphin. The goddess Luna created them." Had no one explained that to Thalasia yet? The way her features settled into understanding confirmed his suspicions. "They pretty much all looked like Nurmoyes. Not that I met anyone outside of Nurmoyes. My mother and I were already living here when they joined us a few years ago."

"What was that like?"

Funny. It almost seemed like they'd come full circle. "It was one of those good things. Before their arrival, our village struggled. There wasn't always enough food to go around. We occasionally lost inhabitants to the mammolisks that came into the grounds. Things changed once they moved here. There were fewer attacks. Crops grew without issue. Water flowed freely. And we got this wall built."

"So, a lot happened." Thalasia tilted her head. "Do you think any of that resulted from Adoni's power? I mean, it makes sense that's why the warlocks went after the golden sirens."

"That's a question best left for Nurmoyes." The guardian had a much better understanding of the golden sirens. He knew only that they existed and that Adoni's parents were the last the warlocks had taken until a few days ago. Beyond that, his knowledge was seriously lacking.

"Understood."

Urbi frowned, a deep line etching itself between his eyebrows. Why had she asked him that? Wouldn't she know something about Adoni's power? Weren't they both sirens? They both had wings, but neither of them had similar appearances. "What about your powers? I've never seen anything like them. Aren't you a siren similar to Adoni?"

"Not exactly."

"I don't understand." Nurmoyes had shared little with him regarding Thalasia. Her lips pressed together in a slight grimace. Had he put her off somehow? Was it rude of him to ask? "I'm sorry if that came out wrong. I just want to know more about you."

She shook her head slightly, a soft puff of air escaping her lips as she blew out a heavy breath. "It's okay, really. We, uh... one of the first things I learned was to be mindful of what's revealed. But I enjoy talking to you."

Well, that worked to his advantage. "I feel the same way." He left it at that. If he dared to press harder, her response would be an icy wall. Each breath he took felt like a burst of sunlight. Space promising the symphony of her voice, which he cherished.

"The goddess who created my species made us in the image of a siren. I possess some of their abilities, but my power far exceeds that. Every part of my arsenal is so I can fight for others. That's out entire purpose."

Her voice, though pleasant, echoed like a siren's call, leading him deeper into the fog of uncertainty. It was if she had answered his question, leaving him more confused than before. "So, you're a siren, but not a siren?"

"Pretty much." Thalasia flashed a knowing smile, her lips curving in a way that suggested she held a secret. One that she'd never completely share.

Maybe that was for the best. If he knew the truth, Nurmoyes could get it out of him. No, if Nurmoyes wanted answers, then they had to seek those out themselves. Urbi stared out across the night sky, lost in its silent and infinite expanse. He liked Thalasia too much to share what he'd discovered.

A comfortable silence stretched between them. Together, they shoulder-to-shoulder, gazing at the vast starlit heavens. The wind whistled, ruffling the short ends of his hair and gently whipping Thalasia's blue tresses loose. Maybe this was the quiet before the storm, but he'd take it as long as he got to spend it with her. It would be something to help him weather the storm when it came.

Because it always came.

That was the price of freedom.

Seven

Nurmoyes swung their blade overhead. It connected with a loud clank to the babian's sword. As they stepped back for another attack, they blasted the babian with a ball of water from a nearby trough. The creature flew backward, landing on the ground with a thud. Their gaze drifted across the grisly battlefield. Their breath stopped, halting in their chest, freezing them in place as they tracked the unfolding chaos.

Several of the draconis howled in frightening joy as those creatures backed away from a group of unmoving soldiers. Nurmoyes narrowed their gaze at the pale faces. Faces they recognized. That they'd trained and fought alongside for years now. *Goddess, those are our people.* It couldn't be. A pool of blood, thick and dark, spread beneath the bodies, its metallic scent hanging heavy in the air. It belonged to the hunters or collectors. Not anyone from their encampment. Forcing themselves to look away, they searched the madness for others—Thalasia, Najjar, or any of their warriors.

A whoosh resounded as something came barreling at them. They sidestepped the iron-tipped arrow. It flew past and embedded in a tall wooden post a few feet behind them. That was far too close for their—with a keening cry, a babian charged full force at them. The edge of the creature's blade clattered against their own. They hadn't finished the enemy off when given the chance. A mistake they wouldn't make again.

Tightening their grip on the hilt, Nurmoyes balled up their fist and swung hard, hitting their opponent in the face. Although the creature's head jerked back, it only pushed more on where their swords had connected. They had to get them loose. Shake them off somehow. So they could get back into the fray. Others needed their help to win this battle.

Everything was on the line, with far too much at stake. The culmination of their struggle over the last few days rested entirely on this last besieged city. They had to reclaim that last pivotal place—the key to everything—before they launched their daring rescue of Adoni. Losing wasn't an option. Drawing their fist back, the guardian thrust outward. The babian dodged the hit, moving its head to the side before their fist connected with its cheek. With a loud hiss, it bared its teeth and sank its fangs into Nurmoyes's forearm.

A howl of pain left their mouth as the babian ripped a chunk of flesh from their arm. Gouts of blood gushed out, splattering them both with a warm, sticky spray. Not that either seemed to care. Survival was all that mattered. Seething with rage, Nurmoyes summoned a gurgle of water from the trough. Without budging an inch, the watery hollow wrapped around the babian's head, covering its nose and mouth.

The creature struggled, gasping for air that wouldn't come. Its hold loosened. The blade fell, clattering against the ground. As the babian stumbled backward, it clawed at the makeshift mask. Not that it accomplished anything. The more it fought, the more difficult each breath became, until it took its last, rattling gasp and collapsed to the ground with a thud.

Nurmoyes didn't relish the kill, but in war one couldn't always avoid it. They'd done what was necessary to protect their companions. The battle hadn't ended yet. Pivoting on the ball of their foot, they turned toward the ongoing fights. There were so many happening at once. Their gaze flitted from one to the next. How could they help? Where did they even begin?

A sickening pop resounded above all the other din, echoing loudly in their ears as if it had occurred right in front of them. Their pale eyes snapped toward the noise. Several feet away, Thalasia stood with her arm flopping loosely and a small blade embedded in her right wing. If they didn't know better, it appeared as if the draconis she fought against had popped her shoulder out of its socket. That was the least of their concerns.

Their pale gaze locked on the gleam of steel coming down in an arc toward her. Nurmoyes jumped into the skirmish, closing the short distance between them. As they lifted their arm without hesitation, they braced for impact. The weapon connected just below the elbow, a wet, tearing sound accompanying the rending of flesh and bone.

A bolt of lightning struck the creature down. Bearing a blank stare, the draconis crumbled to the ground. "What did you do?" Thalasia screamed as she rushed to their side. She tore the thin fabric from her shirt and wrapped the garment around their arm.

"What are you... Why are..." Nurmoyes blinked as blood quickly stained the cotton material. Crap. This wasn't happening. Except the bright-red color clearly indicated the inaccuracy of that assessment. Their gaze swung wide, taking in every part of the ongoing battle. Swords clashed. Fists flew. No matter how hard they fought, they were losing. If they allowed this to continue, it would cost more than the destruction that already stained the earth. "We need to retreat."

"What? No!" Thalasia protested. "We're nearly—"

"Look around!" They gestured at the chaos happening around them. "We've lost people," Nurmoyes admitted. That blood hadn't belonged to the enemy. It belonged to their people. Their soldiers. "And it is only worsening. They were prepared for us this time. We need to retreat." The young female protested vehemently, but it was still the right move.

Her head swiveled one way and then the other. "But..." Thalasia started. Her words fell short. "We're so close."

"We will try again, but not right now." Once they had a better plan, they could reclaim Cragstorm. This wasn't that moment. Before the teenager could argue some more, Nurmoyes yelled, "Retreat! Retreat!"

They may have lost this battle, but that didn't mean the war was over. Far from it. They hadn't come this far just to fail. Not when so many still needed their help. Tomorrow was another day, another chance for them to fight. That mattered more than winning right then. Hopefully, Thalasia saw that. If not, then they'd help her understand this was the right move.

For now.

Adoni stared at the heavy wooden door as it shut behind the female who'd spent hours washing her. From what she'd gathered from the warlocks' earlier conversation, this was part of their ritual. One she couldn't let happen. For days she'd stared at these stone walls, searching for an escape—her eyebrows furrowed as her feathers ruffled. Something wasn't right. Her body didn't feel so weighed down. She slowly stretched her wings, nearly to their full twelve-foot breadth.

Holy crap.

The dark-haired female must've forgotten to put the chains back on her wings. This might be her only chance to get out of here. If she didn't, everything she and Nurmoyes had done over the years would be for naught. Adoni listened, focusing on every little clink of a chain and creak of leather. Waiting seemed like a bad idea, but if she moved too quickly and they caught her, they'd ensure nothing like this ever happened again. At least not before they were ready to steal her power.

Her breath abated as nothing reached her. Not the echoes of footsteps, the crack of a whip, or even the skitter of little feet. There was nothing. The breath she'd held released. Her gaze lifted to the manacles around her wrists. Nothing locked the chains to the hook she hung from, which meant with a slight push... Adoni peered around the four stone walls. She couldn't extend her wings to their full span, but enough that she could get off the hook.

That was only half the battle.

Stretching her wings as far as possible, Adoni gave one good flap and grimaced at the sound of clinking chains as she levitated off the ground. Crap. She hadn't meant to knock things around. Not that she could help it. Not that anyone seemed to notice. Carefully, Adoni extracted the iron from the hook and lowered herself to the ground. "Gods," she moaned.

Immediate relief washed over her wrists and body. This was the first time she'd stood on her own two feet in days.

No time to celebrate.

While she'd love to revel in just this small step, she had to move on before this opportunity slipped through her fingers. Adoni studied the wrought-iron lock. This wasn't something her powers would help with. They didn't work like that. If she had better control over her siren abilities, it might be an option, except she imagined that would draw too much attention. That left one option. She plucked two quills from her wing on a squeaked exhale. *Crap. That hurt.*

The one time she'd seen her parents do that, they'd made it look so easy. It definitely was anything but the sort. Rolling her shoulders, Adoni focused on the task at hand. If she wasn't careful, the sharp end of the quills would snap, screwing up the lock's mechanisms, and she'd be stuck in here forever.

As she worked, her heart raced, a frantic drum against her ribs, an insistent rhythm she could almost hear. The gears resisted, and even the slightest inch of movement took an eternity. No amount of time had ever ticked by so torturously slow. It didn't help that she kept pausing because even the smallest sound convinced her someone had come down that empty corridor. Just when she couldn't take it any longer, the lock clinked, and the door swung open with a faint creak.

Adoni blinked. She'd done it. Holy crap, she'd gotten it open. An icy dread seeped in, silencing any impulse to cheer. Peering through the slight crack, she ensured no one came from either direction and lingered by the jamb for only a moment. Which way did she go? The warlocks had always come from the right. If she went left, that would take her deeper into the dungeons, not toward an exit. So, the way to freedom was toward the warlocks. *Right. That isn't a bad idea.*

Her feet shuffled as she started forward, heading down the narrow, winding passage. Stone surrounded her on both sides. Though she passed a few empty chambers, the flickering light from the torches offered her little aid in deciphering the right direction. She took the next turn only to find herself at a dead end. *Crap.* Shaking the disappointment off, Adoni turned around and continued on. There had to be a way out of this maze. No matter how many corridors she had to go down or how many dead ends she found, she'd get out.

"What the fuck?!"

Those three words rumbled off in the not-so-far distance. The voice sent chills down her spine. A warlock had discovered her prison empty. "No, no, no," Adoni muttered. This wasn't happening. She was so close to escaping. It wasn't going down like this. Ignoring all the sounds that followed that statement, Adoni bolted. She ran as fast as her feet would carry her, taking turn-after-turn. A bright light shone ahead.

The air vibrated with a thunderous boom behind her, each tremor threatening to crumble the very foundations of her courage. As she peered over her shoulder, a large snout came around the corner. The mammolisk's enormous paws kicked up dirt from the floor with every step it took. Her brown gaze flicked briefly toward what she presumed was the exit. Although she knew it would likely catch her, she still had to risk it. Twirling on her toes, she burst toward the radiant light, her heart soaring with the promise of unbounded possibilities.

Her wing throbbed, a searing line of fire crawling through her veins, paralyzing her with dread. Escape was almost within reach. Her breath hitched, each inhale a shallow, ragged struggle against the crushing pressure on her chest. Adoni screamed, a raw, desperate sound. Her jaw clenched, a bitter taste in her mouth, as the encroaching darkness snuffed out the last embers of hope.

Thalasia scrubbed under her nail-beds, but no matter how hard she went at it, she couldn't get Nurmoyes's blood off her skin. Why wouldn't her hands come clean? It was her fault the guardian had gotten hurt. That they'd lost part of their limb. They'd stepped in to protect her... save her. It always happened like that. As much as she tried to keep everyone safe, anyone who helped always suffered because of her actions. Her choices.

They would not save Adoni.

The warlocks would steal the female's power, do whatever they wanted, and take over the realm.

All because she'd failed.

Tossing the cloth into the basin, she pressed her palms to the sink's edge and hung her head. What the fuck was wrong with her? Why did she keep letting this happen? Taking a deep breath in and slowly letting it out, Thalasia tried to calm down as she lifted her eyes to her reflection, the image staring back at her. It didn't help. Her reflection offered no solace, only the haunting vision of bodies scattered throughout the devastated village. The place was a horrifying mess, with limbs and other body parts strewn about. The ground bled red from the amount of loss it held within its arms. She balled up her fist and drove it into the mirror. With a loud crash, glass exploded, showing the stone floor with glittering fragments.

"What did the mirror ever do to you?"

Glancing over her shoulder, she eyed Nurmoyes as they leaned against the jamb. *Great.* The last thing she wanted was to be scolded by the guardian. That's what happened when you forgot to shut the bathroom door behind you. "What do you want?"

"I came to check on you. However, I see the mirror has told you exactly what you needed to hear. Or perhaps they said something you disliked. Judging by your reaction, the latter must be accurate."

"I'm still in one piece." Thalasia bit her tongue. Motherfucker. What was wrong with her? Why would she utter something so insensitive and asinine? *Just kill me now.* Her gaze flicked toward the ceiling. There was no response. Of course not. It was too much to expect the gods to intervene or even to answer her request.

"Is that the problem? Are you upset because I lost part of my arm?"

Not exactly. It was one thing if it had just happened in battle, but it was something else entirely with how it all went down. She should've gotten hurt. Her wing would've taken the brunt because of her own stupidity. As she deserved. She'd taken on the draconis. Not Nurmoyes. Not any of the other soldiers. Her. They suffered because of her choices.

Nurmoyes pushed off the doorway and stepped farther into the room. "Oh, I see. You blame yourself."

"It *is* my fault!" Thalasia snapped, the sound sharp in the air, as she spun around to face them. "You stepped in to save me, and if you hadn't done that, then your arm would still be whole." How could they not see that? It wasn't complex. Nice and simple.

"Perhaps, but you have no way of knowing that for certain. You do not know everything, Thalasia. Even with your gift of sight, every action isn't predictable. You cannot foresee every result or outcome. Let's say that I hadn't interfered. Do you know if someone else wouldn't have done the same?"

"Of course not." It wasn't as if she'd accounted for the whereabouts of all their soldiers. Her focus had remained on both the enemy and the fight. She'd tracked mostly their movements and kept a small visual on where everyone else had ended up. Mostly so they wouldn't get caught in her assaults. Not that she could recall any of that right then. "And the three that died? I suppose that's not on me, either. Although I knew this town would take more effort and they had more time to prepare for our attack. We should've been smarter about it. Come at them in waves, instead of all at once." All things she'd thought about *after* they'd retreated to the compound.

"They were casualties of war." Nurmoyes let out a soft, weary sigh of exasperation, their shoulders slumping slightly. "We all knew what we were getting ourselves into. No amount of preparation or alternate plans will ever alter that. The results outweighed the risks. A decision that each soldier made and accepted themselves. Do not take that honor from them by placing the blame on yourself. You didn't make any choices for us. We did that on our own because we believed you would lead us to victory."

How could they say that? They hadn't won. They'd lost. Runaway when they accepted the inevitable—that if they didn't, they'd all die. That was the antithesis of victory. "Except I haven't. I've failed to lead you anywhere."

"That's inaccurate. With you at the helm, we've accomplished more in the last few days than we have in decades. This town has gone from a sanctuary to a full-blown resistance. Those that we've liberated... more from those villages join us in the fight to reclaim our realm every day. You've given the people hope, Thalasia. *That* is your victory."

Thalasia stared at those pale eyes, searching for any kind of disbelief in what they stated. The guardian's gaze contained nothing save pure conviction, a resolute and unyielding fire. Nurmoyes believed every word. "But you lost part of your arm."

"And that was my choice. A choice I would make every single time. Because it would keep you safe. That matters." The corner of their mouth lifted, hinting at amusement. "Besides, it hasn't taken me out. I'm still quite adept with a sword."

The guardian didn't make a lick of sense. Not only did they not fault her for their injury, they didn't blame her for the lives lost, either. She was the one who'd led them into battle. How was it not all on her? "None of this would've happened if I hadn't shown up here."

"How can you be certain of that?"

"I…" Her words trailed off. As much as she wanted to say she knew it was true, she couldn't. A mammolisk had come for Adoni before she'd even arrived in the village. From what she'd seen, collectors and hunters would've eventually come for Nurmoyes. She didn't know what would've occurred if she hadn't shown up when she had.

"Well, I'm pleasantly surprised you finally understand that." Nurmoyes cracked a grin. "Thalasia, you can't control the actions and reactions of those around you. You only control your own. That is what you must focus on. Although I didn't see it at first, you are exactly what we needed. Now, if you're ready, we have some wounded who require healing. We've got a war to finish."

Right. Her visions were only one of many potential outcomes. Not written in stone. The gods sent her to change them in any way she could. While she'd done that, she wasn't done yet. Thalasia glanced back at the sink and shut off the water. She'd deal with the mess later. Right now, she had work to do. "Let's give 'em hell."

Whistling, Drach wiped the blood from his hands with a semi-clean rag. A malicious smile crossed his face as he eyed the welts and bruises blooming all over the siren's body, each mark a canvas of violence. This would teach her a harsh lesson she wouldn't soon forget, deterring another run. Something that shouldn't have happened in the first place. When he discovered who'd forgotten to chain his golden siren's wings, well, they'd hurt like hell for it.

"Aw, hell!" Nox exclaimed. "Come on. How are we supposed to drain her like this?" His brother gestured to the broken body hanging from the steel hook.

It wasn't as if he'd killed the female. The guy should be grateful he'd shown such restraint. No way Kaspar would've done the same. "Give her a couple of days to heal on her own. Whatever is still lingering, we can deal with." It would also give them time for answers regarding the unexplained shift and information regarding the female who helped the opposition. Plus, they still needed the siren's guardian.

A groan escaped Nox as he scrubbed a weary hand down his stubbled face. "I'm going to pretend those words didn't just escape your lips." The male stepped aside, making room for Lapa to join the conversation. "Tell him what you just told me."

The draconis bowed his head to both of them and directed his attention to Drach. "My lord, we believe the continuum disruption and the female aiding the opposing forces are related."

"Really?" Didn't that just get the blood stirring. A warm rush through his veins. With a flick of his wrist, he tossed the rag aside, folded his arms across his chest, and leaned against his workbench, the wood cool against his back. "How so?"

"The female is a blue-haired, blue-winged creature. She looks like a siren, but possesses mystical traits we've never seen before."

Alright. His fists tightened at his sides, a burning rage simmering within him as the male spoke. He shouldn't have to prompt continuation of any kind. "Such as?"

"She holds bolts of white light in her hands and uses them to kill draconis. We've also discovered remnants of many corpses of warriors, collectors, hunters, and their... pets."

With a quick glance at his brother, Drach's eyebrows raised in silent question. It all sounded impossible, but if the vibrant excitement shining out of Nox's eyes was anything to go by, it was entirely accurate. This suggested the female was even more powerful than the golden siren, who hung limply like a discarded piece of meat. A slow smile spread across Drach's face. "Well, Lapa, it appears you have a female to catch. Alive."

"Yes, my lord." The male bowed his head and left.

"Do you think he'll find and capture her?" Nox posed once they were alone. "Or that she's truly related to the issue with the continuum?"

Those were both valid questions. To the first well, if Lapa wished to keep his life, the male would succeed. As for the second, that required a lot of theorizations. "It's possible." Drach dipped his chin toward the golden siren. "We don't exactly know where they came from. Just that they arrived along with their guardians, giving us what we've always needed."

"What's that?"

"Opportunity." The power they demanded required a heavy toll. A sacrifice that matched their desires. And it was nearly complete.

T halasia paced back and forth, kicking up grains of sand with each step she took. Gods, this was beyond boring. Her gaze flicked once more toward the spot she'd left Nurmoyes. This wasn't supposed to take forever. Maybe she wasn't the best choice for bait, after all. She lingered as close to the watchtower as she dared to get. If she got any closer, she might as well hold up a flashing sign that read, *I'm what you're looking for.* Crikey. This was—the light from a lantern flashed twice. "About fucking time," she muttered. Now they could get this show on the road.

Her ears twitched as she listened for the sound of a collector approaching. She slowly eased the dagger from her belt. The point wasn't to kill the thing, but to distract it. An idea that had come from her impatiently waiting for the map to update. Something that hadn't happened. The memory of last night's conversation surfaced.

Nurmoyes stared at her. Their eyebrows drawn together in confusion. "You want to do what?"

"Capture a collector." It seemed like a simple proposal. Though judging by their grim expressions, etched with worry, maybe not. "We failed to retake Cragstorm by going at them directly. You were right. They were prepared for us. No matter what kind of plan we come up with, the same scenario is likely to play out. Which means we need to do something outside the box. Something they'd never expect. Instead of trying to take back the remaining town, we need to go straight for the rescue. We can't do that unless we know

where Adoni is being held. And Urbi told me you have some way of extracting the truth from people. So, if we capture a collector, they can't lie. They have to answer our questions."

"Wow. That's actually pretty smart." Najjar gently smacked Nurmoyes's arm. "Why didn't we think of that? I mean, if we get one of the higher-ups, we could find out all kinds of information."

"Except kidnapping a collector would require patience. We'd have to iden-tify one, and not just any of them would do, especially if you're seeking one with that kind of knowledge. Not to mention, we'd have to be close to Silverspire for this to even work. Even if we went unseen, how would you suggest we draw their attention?"

"Uh, well..." Thalasia cracked a bright, toothy grin and raised a hand. "Me. As bait."

Yeah. Nurmoyes had cared little for that recommendation, but it was better than the alternative. Failing to reclaim the last city wasn't on her agenda. This would work. It had to because if it didn't—a low growl resounded behind her. "Just what I was looking for," the draconis declared.

Thalasia spun around, facing the creature. "Yeah, well, that makes two of us." Spreading her legs, she lifted her dagger up and waved the fucker forward. "Come on, big boy. Let's see what you've got."

It lunged toward her, and she jumped into the air, leaping over its head as she struck it in the back with the edge of her blade. Just as she landed, Nurmoyes hit the ground directly between her and the draconis. It spun around to face her, and Nurmoyes blew a white powder directly into the draconis's face. The creature waved its hand, batting at the fine substance as it weaved on its feet. She peered around Nurmoyes. Down the draconis went, hitting the ground with a thunk. "Man, that shit works fast."

"Yes, it does."

"And you're certain this is the one we need?" Thalasia gestured to the hulking body. It was going to take a lot for them to get it out of here and back to the compound without getting caught.

"Positive. Check the insignia on its armband." They pointed to the triangular patch with three lines on the dark cloth wound tightly around his biceps. "This is Lapa. Commander of the collectors. He will have all the answers we require." The corner of Nurmoyes's mouth lifted.

"Then let's get out of here before anyone realizes he's missing." Stepping around the guardian, she hooked an arm under the draconis's pits while the guardian got on the other side. "Though… if we have to do this again, you get to be the bait," Thalasia whispered. "I'm tired of spreading my damn pheromones around for these fuckers." The last thing she needed was to leave her scent all over the damn place. Who knew what consequences that would bring? She sure as hell didn't want to find out.

Nurmoyes scrutinized the map of Silverspire that Thalasia had drawn out based on the information they'd collected from Lapa. The male had provided much more than they could've ever hoped for. Not only did they know exactly where Adoni was being held, they had the maze pattern on how to get her out once they rescued her, and where to find the warlocks. "So, we are all in agreement? Thalasia will hit the dungeons with two soldiers, retrieve Adoni, and exit through the tunnels while the rest of us handle the diversion and assault on the warlocks."

"Are you certain about this?" the silver-eyed teenager asked once again.

It was a question she'd posed three times already. Not that their answer altered. "Yes. I am positive." They had to come at this from three different directions. The group on the outside would draw the warlocks out of hiding while serving as a diversion so she could access the dungeons without incident. Once the warlocks came into the clearing, the coven they'd protected for years came into play. It would prove the ultimate test for everything, but they believed in the power of those females.

With a groan, Thalasia raked her hand through her long, blue locks. "I just don't understand how you can expect to defeat the warlocks without me, your powerhouse."

"That's the purpose of *The Sisters of Serenity*. They have spent decades preparing for this," Najjar stated. "The only way all of this works is if we stick to our parts of the plan."

"Okay, okay." Thalasia rubbed her forehead with her thumb. "Multiple points of attack." She sighed heavily. "I'm just worried it won't be enough. Not just for me to get out with Adoni, but that you all will pay the price."

"Which is why your sole focus is Adoni and getting out through the underground tunnel system. Do you understand, Thalasia? You're not to turn back for us. The only way we all succeed is if you take her straight to your jump point. Are we clear on this?" Because if they got the golden siren out of Bahalah, then no matter what happened from there, they would have defeated the warlocks. The plan of those males was contingent upon stealing Adoni's power. As well as Thalasia's. It was far too important those two to stay far, far away from the battle.

"I get it." Her gaze narrowed at them. "That doesn't mean I have to like it."

No, the female was right about that. Nurmoyes dipped their chin, acknowledging her statement. They understood how she felt. Parts of this bothered them as well, but it was beyond necessary. Najjar continued a recount of the rest of the plan. Not that they heard a single word. Instead, they recalled the last thirteen years of Adoni's life. They had been among the first to hold her outside of her parents. Such a small child with an extremely powerful destiny. Ensuring that succeeded was paramount. Not just in Bahalah, but in other realms in the universe, too. Adoni's parents hadn't been long for this world. Nurmoyes had taught the young female nearly her whole life. Though they'd kept her close, she hadn't learned all she should've. Their gaze lifted from the map as everyone dispersed. "Thalasia, will you stay a moment longer?"

"Yeah, sure."

Silence stretched between them as the last of those gathered left. Even with everyone gone, they still couldn't quite find the words. They had to share this information with her. It was far too important to keep to themselves. Nurmoyes strode across the room and leaned against a wall. The cool stone felt good against their wings. "I suppose by this point you've deduced Adoni is special. Much like you."

"For the warlocks to go through all this, figured she had to be."

"The power of a golden siren develops over the years of its life. Each year until their eighteenth birthday, they become stronger, more powerful, even without using their abilities. This becomes evident in the color of their wings. Right now, Adoni's wings are brown. However, at some point, she will shed those quills, and new golden ones will grow in thcir stead." They focused on Thalasia, studying her reaction as they disclosed the truth of Adoni's existence. And her importance.

For a moment, Thalasia perked up and leaned forward, focusing on them. Her eyebrows furrowed as if she were processing their words. With a slight shake of her head, she frowned. "Okay. I'm confused. What does that have to do with her power? I mean, I know sirens can shoot their quills from their wings. I've done it myself, but I've never heard of a change like that."

"The color changes to match the accurate representation of her abilities." Nurmoyes scratched the back of their neck. It was a roundabout way to explain everything, but they had to give her as much as possible. "When she has reached her full potential, she will be able to locate mystical power sources. Not just one kind. All of them."

Thalasia's silver eyes widened as she stared blankly at them. "Excuse me?"

"You heard me." While her reaction made perfect sense, Nurmoyes hadn't lied. Given the way she stared at them, she understood why it was so imperative they get Adoni out. "As much as I would like to say goodbye to my charge, you must promise me that you will not wait for me at the ruins. You will leave with her."

Her entire body straightened as she pushed off the table. "What?"

"I cannot make this any clearer. If I'm not at the ruins, leave with her. Promise me." If they'd discovered anything about Thalasia over the last few days, it was that she was a female who kept her word. Which was why they demanded she make a promise to them. Perhaps it was wrong to use the teenager's characteristics against her, but they had to prioritize Adoni and Thalasia's safety. Even if it meant letting both of them go without so much as a word. Adoni may never forgive the decision, but they could live with that. As long as Thalasia held up her end of the deal, ensuring Adoni left Bahalah and never came back, then the sacrifice was worth it.

"You can't be serious? All I've heard since I arrived was how Adoni is your responsibility. *Now*, not only do you want to place that on my shoulders, but you want me to convince her we have to leave without a goodbye?"

"There is no other choice." The guardian's sigh hung in the air, heavy with the weight of ages. They didn't require visions to play out all outcomes. "While I have every faith that the coven will succeed, I cannot bank Adoni's safety on that. Your success matters most. As long as the two of you escape, then the warlocks will fail and our realm will survive." Even if they didn't. That went without saying. "I will have fulfilled my duty by ensuring you fill yours."

This hunt ended only one way.

"Kaspar!" Drach roared, beating on the door, his blood boiling as the ear-splitting cries coming from his brother's room fueled his rage. What the fuck was the male doing to his pet? Each pounding blow against the unresponsive door reverberated with unrestrained fury and pent-up resentment. Enough of this. Drach took a step back, then sent a crackling jolt of magic at it, throwing it wide open with a resounding crash.

His gaze fell to his female, slumped against the side the luxurious bed, her breathing shallow and ragged. Blood streaked her face, highlighting the tender, swollen bruises. Blinded by rage, Drach charged across the room; his fist connected with Kaspar's jaw, sending the male crashing into the unforgiving stone wall with a sickening thud. "What the fuck is wrong with you?"

"Tell him," Kaspar hacked out as struggled to his feet.

Whatever his pet had to say didn't matter. It didn't give his brother the right to punish the female. That right belonged to him alone. Drach stormed over to where his brother still struggled to stand, his ragged breaths filling the air. The plush carpet luxuriously cushioned his steps, completely silencing them as he closed the distance between them. He grabbed Kaspar by the throat and with a grunt, slammed the male into the wall, the impact echoing loudly as the stone fractured.

"My liege," his female pled. "It was my error."

"She's how the bitch got out," his brother uttered with a faint, pained groan.

Did they think he hadn't deciphered that for himself? She'd washed that siren on his order. It didn't take a genius to figure out what happened afterward. None of that was the point. Not even the damage he'd dealt out to the siren two days ago.

Kaspar's face contorted in anger as he locked eyes with him, thrashing against Drach's hold. "You fucking knew!"

"Of course, I fucking knew," he whispered as he got in his brother's face, close enough to smell the male's stale breath, and jabbed a finger at him. "And I don't give a fuck! I told you not to lay a finger on her head, but you did it anyway."

Kaspar gripped Drach's forearm and spat out, "Someone had to," the words sharp and angry. "Because I knew you wouldn't."

"Enough!" Nox yelled from the doorway. "We're under siege, and the two of you are acting like petulant children."

His knuckles cracked as he clenched his fist, the sight of his youngest brother barely stemming the burning fire within. *Under siege?* "What the fuck are you talking about?" The opposition couldn't possibly be that mind-numbingly stupid. Taking small, inconsequential villages was one thing, but stepping into their vibrant city, their heart of power, was a deadly game.

"The remaining mutuphin, along with a coven, is within our walls," Nox ground out. "Do you understand?"

Impossible, except the male's golden gaze held nothing but the cold, hard truth. It appeared the day he thought might find them had finally arrived. Something he'd long ago prepared for, just in case. Drach released his brother, and Kaspar fell to the floor with a muffled thud. The male could clean himself up for all he cared. This was nothing more than a temporary reprieve.

So to speak

Drach strode around the dark wood furniture, collected his female into his arms as he eyeballed her injuries, and caressed her cheek with the back of his knuckles. Nothing appeared too serious. "Are you all right, Ayah?"

"Yes, my liege."

Good. It meant she could leave on her own and follow through with their plan. He brushed a soft kiss across her lips, leaned in close, and whispered in her ear, "You know what to do." A slight, almost imperceptible nod of her head was his pet's only acknowledgment. Leaving the three of them behind, she scampered out of the room, her footsteps echoing as she disappeared down the long corridor. Wisely, neither Nox nor Kaspar uttered a single word as the female left. Drach peered between his brothers. "We've got work to do."

With a swift, one-handed swing, Nurmoyes struck the collector's arm; a scattering of shimmering scales fell away from the impact point. Engulfed in the oppressive heat of the fight, they threw whatever they could at the enemy, while the coven unleashed a storm of magic against the three warlocks. Having only half an arm couldn't keep them from this battle. Not with so much on the line.

"Duck!" Arietta hollered.

The guardian silently dropped onto their haunches, eyes never leaving their target. A fireball hissed past, the smell of sulfur stinging their nostrils as it slammed into the draconis's chest. It was only of many points of magic that crackled and popped, swirling all around them. The creature ran, a loud screech tearing from its throat, its scales smoking as it tried to put out the fire consuming it. As the draconis collapsed to the ground with a sickening crunch, Nurmoyes rose to their full height of six-two and focused intently on the nearby clash of magic.

They turned to thank Arietta, but the warlock, with his short, white hair, interrupted by hurling a crackling stream of fire at the woman. Nurmoyes countered with a forceful water current; the blaze died with a hissing plume of steam. Together, they joined another coven member and launched a simultaneous attack on the warlock.

Though the air crackled as spells flew between the two coven members and the warlock, every blow missed its mark. There had to be something they could do. Just because the guardian possessed little magic didn't mean they couldn't help level the playing field. Maybe they just needed to distract the warlock, then the witches could take the male out without issue.

With sparks crackling along his fingertips, the warlock's face twisted into a malicious grin. Nurmoyes didn't know what the male had planned, but this was their moment. With a surge of power, the guardian unleashed a roaring water stream that slammed into the warlock, immediately grounding his crackling electric charge and causing him to stumble backward, sputtering. As Nurmoyes charged toward the warlock, they spun out at the last second and hollered, "Now!"

The witches combined their mystical powers. Together, the females shot an immense force, accompanied by a sickening wet sound, across the male's neck, decapitating him. His head, with is wide amber eyes staring blankly, fell to the ground with a resounding thud.

One down—"Nurmoyes!" a coven member screamed, her voice shrill, ear-piercing cry over the roar of the ongoing battle. They turned just as the gray-haired warlock disappeared into the castle grounds. *No!* They had no way of knowing if Thalasia had escaped with Adoni yet. Without a second though, Nurmoyes took off after the warlock.

With a grunt, Thalasia shoved her blade into the babian's belly, piercing its flesh. Blood splattered all over her pants and the ground as she kicked it off her sword. How many did that make now? Too fucking many to count. They'd encountered way more problems as they made their way toward Adoni than anyone expected. It had taken far longer than she had wanted.

This was another one to add to the growing trail of bodies they'd left in their wake.

"Let's keep moving." She darted forward. Their shadows bounced off the cylindrical walls, catching in the flickering lights of the torches hanging in the iron sconces. There wasn't much farther for them to go. One more dank passageway and they should arrive at their destination. "Left!" Thalasia hollered over the screaming prisoners as she bolted around the corner with two soldiers hot on her tail. She skidded to a halt in front of the cell holding the siren. "Here," she called out to her companions.

"Let's get it open."

No shit. Without hesitation, she inserted the key they'd stolen from Lapa last night. *Please let this work.* If it didn't, she was about to summon a shitload of lightning to break the fucker open. The gears tumbled as she turned the thick piece of iron. "Oh, thank gods," she muttered. The door swung wide, revealing a bruised and bloodied female with dirty brown hair hanging in the center of the room. Thalasia blinked.

"Holy shit," one guard uttered.

He could say that again. Dear gods, was Adoni even alive? The female's head lolled to one side as her bare feet scraped the dirt. Black and blue covered half of her swollen face. Thalasia swallowed to wet her parched throat. *Please, please don't let me break my promise.* "Help me get her down." There wasn't any time to waste. The four of them had to get moving. Two of them rushed into the dungeon together. She and Hassan eased Adoni from the hook she dangled from. Once they had the female down, Thalasia checked her pulse. A steady rhythm thumped beneath her fingers. That was something.

"You need to heal her," the male stated.

"We don't have time for that. She's alive. To keep her that way, we need to get moving. Once we're far enough away, I can heal her." Not before then. She didn't know how the battle above them fared, and it wasn't as if she could find out.

The female stirred. "Hassan?" One brown-eye opened at half-mast. "What's... happening?" Adoni choked out.

"We're getting you out of here," he replied and swept her dirty hair from her face. Not that it seemed the female noticed. "Come on," he started. "Let's get her on your shoulder. You know how this has to work."

That she did. Damn Nurmoyes for forcing her to agree to it. Thalasia nodded. With the male's help, she lugged Adoni onto her shoulder, who, thankfully, had passed out. It would make transportation that much easier. With one soldier flanking her backside and the other her front, they took off together through the winding corridors going deeper and deeper into the dungeons. Originally, she'd planned for them to release any prisoners they crossed along the way, except there wasn't time for that. The two males would have to backtrack and do it once they parted ways. Another part of the plan that hadn't thrilled her. At least nothing else got in their way as they reached the tunnels. Sweat trickled down into her eyes as the large, round infrastructure came into view.

"Thank you," one soldier stated as the two males stopped at the entrance's mouth. "Now, go. Fly like you've never flown before."

"Be safe." Without looking back, Thalasia hitched Adoni a little higher on her shoulder and took off. According to what they'd learned from Lapa, these pathways led directly out of the city. Once she hit the exit, she left everything behind and headed straight to the sky. Wind whipped her hair from her face as she flew like their lives depended on it. Because it did.

Even with the heat of the sun's rays beating down on her back, she made it to the ruins in record time. Adoni didn't rouse once throughout the flight. Hopefully, the female came around after she healed her. If Nurmoyes didn't show up before that point, well, a promise was a promise. They wouldn't wait. They would leave. Without question.

Spotting the weather-worn pillars from the sky, Thalasia dove toward the sturdiest stone she saw. She needed a safe place to lay Adoni down so she could tend to the female's injuries. Chalky dust got up in her nose as she touched down near a couple of faceless marble statues. There was no telling who they used to be; not even by the garb the forms wore. Thalasia located the only shaded spot and carefully set Adoni on a large block of cracked stone.

They hadn't bothered with the shackles around the female's wrists. Digging into the pocket of her loose pants, she retrieved the key, unlocked the chains, and tossed them aside. Really, she should destroy them, but healing came first. Hovering her hand above Adoni's chest, Thalasia allowed the silver light to pour from her into the siren's body. Inch by inch, centimeter by centimeter, the siren's flesh knitted together. The bruises disappeared.

The pale color of her skin slowly returned. Within a matter of minutes, it appeared as if none of it had ever happened.

"Is she alive?"

Thalasia's head swiveled. Her gaze snapped toward the voice that came from behind her. A grin settled across her face. As the last of her magic worked its way through, she gestured toward Adoni. "See for yourself."

The female's brown eyes fluttered open. "Nurmoyes?" Her voice came out meekly, almost like a soft breeze.

"Oh, thank Luna," Nurmoyes said as they dropped to their knees next to the young siren. "You're alive."

"Am I?" Tears welled in the corners of Adoni's eyes, trickling down her cheeks.

"Yes, alive and safe."

"Really?" Adoni's gaze darted back and forth, scrutinizing Nurmoyes's face as if she were searching for a lie. Her eyes fell on Thalasia. "You. You're the one they asked me about."

"I imagine I am." Now that everything was as it should be, they had to get moving. It would take them several minutes to get to the actual jump point. She leaned down. "Nurmoyes, I hate to say this, but—"

"You must go."

"Yep."

"Go? Go where?" Adoni asked. "Where are you going? Why are you going? What's going on?"

"I will explain everything." Nurmoyes helped Adoni to her feet. Their pale eyes swing in Thalasia's direction. "Perhaps you should change before your departure."

As she checked out the mess of her attire, she nodded. Yep, she wasn't just covered in blood, but guts, too. At least she hoped that's what it was. "Talk to her while I do that. You've got two minutes." Thalasia turned around, scanning their surroundings for a semi-decent place to change.

"Of course," the guardian started. "And Thalasia... one got away."

Motherfucker. She didn't want to know that. That wasn't part of the plan. They were supposed to have killed all three warlocks while she rescued Adoni. Not a single one was supposed to escape. With a slight dip of her chin, Thalasia strolled forward. This would come back to haunt them. There wasn't anything she could do about it at the moment. Not until she got Adoni safely to a sanctuary realm. Afterward, well, that depended on the gods. For all she knew, they could intend this as another problem for another day. Though she hoped not.

It seemed smarter to resolve the issue all at once. Not leave it and pray it didn't bite you in the ass. That was what she had to do. For now.

Nine

"Again!" Nira shouted. All four of her bushy tails flicked back and forth as she stood there, watching Chase run the obstacle course for the tenth time, her eyes intently following his every move. Whoever thought it was a brilliant idea for a kitsune to train a dragon-shifter had clearly lost their marbles. Especially when there was such an age difference between them. But it was certainly necessary.

Although she was the guardhian of this realm, he served as her prohtector. Without learning to summon his powers while human, how could he possibly protect her from harm? She tapped her chin and mentally ran through the obstacle course she'd built. Hmm, perhaps if she altered the illusion her so-called prohtector currently ran, then she might see some progress.

With a groan, Chase rolled his eyes and stomped off, zigzagging through the trees until he reached the course's starting point. "This would be so much easier if I could just do it in my other form."

"You need to do this in both forms. You're stronger than you give yourself credit for; your dragon form isn't necessary to run this course." Even his much larger and fierier side, with all its bluster, couldn't resolve every problem. He had to master it in his human form first, and then they could focus more on his dragon.

"Perhaps if you allow him to run it once in his desired form, he will find it easier to complete in his current form."

Her gaze lifted to the catalync half-curled on a nearby branch. Most of the time, Ahmya had excellent suggestions. This wasn't one of those moments. Nira tilted her head and looked over the dark-blue furry creature with the spiked tail. Really, catalyncs were intended as guides as she performed her guardhian duties. Things she needed to know to keep the realm protected, and its inhabitants safe from harm. Her face bloomed with delight as a wide, genuine smile stretched across it. "Maybe he just needs a little encouragement."

The cat-like creature stretched its back and slunk forward, draping a paw off the branch. "You cannot possibly think that will work."

"Well…" She bobbed her head from side to side. Really, there were only two options. One, he saved Ahmya from certain death without resorting to his dragon form, or two, he failed, and she died. "I suppose it could fail, in which case, he'd have let you die."

"Either way, it certainly makes me grateful it is nothing more than an illusion."

Therein lay the problem. As long as Chase believed failure didn't equate to death, he risked nothing with his consistent defeat. Nira grinned widely. It was time to change the game and up the ante. "Don't be so sure about that."

"Am I running this again or are you two going to sit there and chitchat some more?" Chase hollered.

"You wouldn't!" Ahmya's green eyes bulged.

Snapping her fingers, she transported the catalync to a thickly layered net hanging from a branch and created a new goal for her prohtector. From the ground, a *yokai* jumped in the air, clutching its jaws as it attempted to rip the net open and enjoy a tasty, yet furry, treat. While she couldn't actually summon such a demonic animal with dark scales, a large maw, and razor-sharp teeth, it appeared genuine enough. Especially as Ahmya played the part well of a frightened catalync and dug her claws into the net to climb it from the inside, only to slide back down.

Nira focused her attention on Chase, whose eyes had widened in horror. She opened her mouth, and before any words could escape, he darted into the silent forest, leaped over gnarled roots, swung effortlessly from mossy branches, and charged into the fray prepared to fight with a fierce roar. Finally.

The male moved with great speed and agility; she actually lost sight of him twice. He disappeared behind the vibrant maple tree, its leaves a kaleidoscope of color, then became one with the purple Wysteria leaves dangling low. Talk about impressive. Not only had he pulled on his dragon strength, but he'd even activated some of his powers. Did he even realize what he'd accomplished in this small amount of time?

Typical *yokai* couldn't be killed with just any type of weapon. If this had been a real demonic animal, then it would've only been able to be destroyed by a *taijiya* or Buddhist monk. Of course, neither accounted for the sleek blade Chase carried at his hip, or the dagger on the other side. Both contained magical powers that would devour any demon it encountered; one even created in an illusion.

With as fast as Chase moved, if she didn't throw a few surprises in the mix, he'd get to the catalync in record time and destroy a non-existent demonic creature. Just before his hand released from a branch, the tree he aimed for disappeared. It required him to react without slowing to analyze the options in front of him. Crossing her arms, Nira stepped over a nearby root and stared as he shifted direction and clambered up the tree.

Stepping forward, she tracked his movements as he crawled from one tree to another and found a way around the rushing river. He got to the other side where the *yokai* still jumped in the air, getting closer and closer to its furry prize. While she could throw another wrench in whatever he planned, she decided against it. Instead, she wanted to see how he would go about the rescue. Would he come in fast and strong? Or would he... a smile crossed her face as he went for option two.

He utilized his dragon powers and disappeared into the dark green of the lush forest. Her eyes bounced around as she anticipated the best route for him to take through the treetops, which meant he'd come barreling down on the lizard-type creature at an angle and... Just as she predicted, Nira caught sight of the gleaming blade as it sliced through the head of the *yokai*.

Chase cut the netting and set Ahmya free.

Her smile was radiant, and the sound of her clapping hands made the illusion disappear, revealing the beauty of the real world. "Now, that is what I call a successful mission."

"You hung me from a tree." The catalync glowered at her.

"Are you certain about that?" Nira tilted her head and clasped her hands together at the small of her back. It amused her to mess with her guide... sometimes, anyway.

Thalasia dragged a hand through her blue hair as fog rolled across their feet. This was one thing she despised about where this jump point was located. It was already terrifying trekking through the ancient, hallowed ruins, but the clammy mist snaking from the earth chilled her to the bone. That was before they even made it underground, where they'd trek through dank tunnels to get to the actual jump point. Of course, she'd already gone through this once a few days ago. She wouldn't have returned except it was the only way out.

She glanced over her shoulder at the siren that stayed tight on her heels. The young female peered all around as they made their way through the darkened path toward their exit. While she didn't blame her for sticking close by, if the siren got any closer, she'd be up her ass.

With a heavy sigh, Thalasia turned her attention back to the stone trail lit by nothing more than torches hanging on the walls. This was the fifth tunnel they had to walk through, about thirty feet below the ground. The builders constructed these ruins in such a way that they were solid and echoed the sounds of the past. A multitude of staircases and tunnels; some of which led to a central cavern, while others led to pits. The sound of her boots clicking against the cold, hard earth reverberated in the underpass.

"Are we almost there?" Adoni asked as she grabbed onto Thalasia's arm.

If she hadn't seen the hidden language of her people along the way, she'd almost believe they'd been going in the wrong direction. And if the signs were accurate, they should hit the cavern with the jump point soon. "Yes."

"Okay. Good."

She offered the girl a soft smile, her fingers gently patting Adoni's hand. The girl might physically only be a couple of years younger than her, but their education levels differed. Maybe if she gave the female an idea of what to expect, it might ease her some. "Listen, we'll be approaching an enormous cavern here shortly. You'll see a lot that won't make sense, but trust me... getting you away from the warlock was only the first step. The second is getting you out of this realm."

"Realm? You said that earlier. I do not understand."

That always seemed to be a term that confused many. With all the people she'd rescued over the last few years, it wasn't something that had gotten easier to explain. "This place, Bahalah, is considered a realm. While this is the world you have known all thirteen years you've been alive, there are other species or creatures that live and exist in other worlds. Some may be similar or completely different from what you've grown up around."

"You mean, more warlocks?"

Thalasia opened her mouth and snapped it shut. Of course, the female would worry about that. While they existed in other realms, it probably wasn't best to share that information and have Adoni fear where they were about to go. "You don't have to worry about them anymore. I'm taking you to a safe place. It's what we call a sanctuary realm."

"Sanctuary? What does that mean?"

"It means you'll have a chance to grow up and thrive." She'd already told the female it would be a safe place. While she could think of several other ways to describe it, that seemed like the best possible answer.

"Really? Will there be other sirens that live there?"

That was a tough question. Well... sort of. She hadn't found a lot of information in her ancestor's journal that spoke much about the other realm—one of the many things that annoyed her about that damn thing. It was supposed to contain a lot of useful material. That wasn't always the case. Thalasia sighed. "I wish I could tell you yes, Adoni, but as far as I know, you'll be the only siren. That may change in the future, but for now, the other species that live there will be your companions."

"Oh." The female's brown eyes flicked toward the ground as they entered a large, circular cavern.

Pausing mid-step, she turned and faced Adoni. Thalasia squeezed the young siren's hands. "Listen, things may be awkward at first, but I promise that An Talamh Lus is a place where you'll be free to live how you choose."

Adoni's gaze lifted. "Really?"

"Yes." If everything she'd read about the place held true, then this girl would actually find her freedom there. Though it would take time to get past a life of running. It was all that this girl had ever known. In some small way, she understood. Not because their lives were similar, at least not in most ways, but because she knew what it was like to be tied to something without a choice.

Shaking her thoughts away, Thalasia peered over her shoulder at the various inscriptions embedded in the stone floor, and then squeezed Adoni's hand one last time. "You ready? Because we need to go."

With a brief nod, a faint smile crossed the girl's face. "Yes. I am ready."

"Then follow me." Keeping their hands linked, she led the siren toward the middle of the cavern. It wasn't hard to spot the divide in the terrain, forming a series of connected rings, like a portal beckoning her forward. Well, it did for someone who knew the combination, so to speak. "Now, whatever you do, don't let go of my hand, and touch nothing. If you reach out to anything shiny as we jump from this realm to the next, it will hurt and cause damage. Got it?"

"I understand."

"Good." She prayed the female listened. Only one person failed to heed her warning in the past, and they lost a finger as a result. Given how little Adoni had experienced in her life, she didn't think it would be something she had to worry over.

Standing in the cavern's heart, Thalasia gazed at each stone wall, the echoes of her breath bouncing back. The smooth rock, worn by ages of wind and rain, offered no purchase for navigation, making it nearly impossible to find north. The etching on the ground saved them. She got the two of them situated, and then pulled out the golden lyre that hung from a chain around her neck. Focusing on the narrow strings and the lines around the edge that represented wings, it lit up. The stone rings around them shifted, each one repositioning with a loud click and settling until the complex symbols shone a bright gold. The last ring locked in place, and the glow from the lyre engulfed them, shooting them through a prismatic gateway.

One second, they were in a cold hollow, and the next they'd flown through a multicolored portal in a haze and reappeared in a lush forest. As they arrived, a wave of energy rolled through the area, causing the purple leaves to ripple and dance in the wind.

The three of them had started toward the main cabin, cracking a few jokes about how frightened Ahmya had appeared. A hard wind pushed at their backs, flapping her ears and tails wildly. Nira glanced over her shoulder toward the source of the distant blast, then turned to meet the worried gazes of her companions. "Did you feel that?"

"Yes," Chase said.

Ahmya nodded to the two of them. "Both of you go."

"Head on to the cabin." Giving her prohtector the go-ahead, Nira shifted to her animal form. It made the most sense for Ahmya to continue without them. Although catalyncs had spiked tails, they were more intellectual creatures than anything else. The female could defend herself, but she'd also be slow moving as well.

Without waiting for Chase—it would take him a moment longer to shift and get into the air—she took off and raced in the direction she'd sensed the gust. Like the human world, storms still passed through here, but this didn't feel like anything natural. She couldn't quite describe how it had felt, except it made her skin crawl.

Nira ran as fast as her legs could carry her, which in this form was almost like driving a car on a highway. It wasn't long before she felt a burst of wind from above her, which was a good thing. It meant Chase was finally on the move. She didn't want their position given away. She didn't know what had entered her realm, or how, but whatever it was, she wanted to sneak up on it.

This had been one of the many reasons she had Chase train as much as she did. In case something like this ever happened. She pushed her body harder, leaped over gnarled, sprawling roots, hustled around overgrown trunks covered in moss, and bounded across huge, scratchy bushes. Having lived in the realm for hundreds of years, she knew the forest like she knew her own fur. She skidded to a stop and lifted her muzzle in the air. Whatever creature... no, wait, creatures... had found their way to An Talamh Lus, they smelled... strange. Unlike anything she'd ever sensed before.

Their scents were light and airy, barely there but still noticeable. That rang true for one. It was a bit of a soft, floral aroma. The other one was a deep, woody scent with a sweet accent. What could these creatures possibly be? The two smells had carried on the breeze, but they weren't nearby. Jumping through the brambles, she darted off and followed their aromas. Maybe she wouldn't find them exactly, but there was no doubt in her mind she'd locate their entry point.

That was okay. They would discover them at some point. That was why Chase flew overhead, above the treetops. It gave her the opportunity to catch their magical essence. Then she could tell exactly what had come into the realm—one of the many benefits of being a celestial kitsune. She could see things that others couldn't. Provided she could identify the essence. Even at her age, she didn't know everything.

As she approached a small clearing, she slowed her pace. Nira tilted her head and sniffed the air. She could see what remained of the magical lines, like shimmering dust motes in the air. This was definitely where they'd come in, but she didn't recognize either spirit. Whatever power had been used to bring them here, it was something powerful. And old. Huh.

Her gaze flicked to the tall trees covered in deep-purple leaves. What could these things be? And where had they gone?

Ten

Thalasia peered through the leaves on the tree she and Adoni had used as a hiding spot. It hadn't been the greatest of ideas, but upon entering the new realm, she knew she had to glimpse its keeper to get a sense of its power. If she had to take a bet, she'd go with the fox studying their entrance point as this realm's keeper. Which also meant it had to be more just an ordinary fox. Judging from the larger appearance and multiple tails, it was likely a kitsune.

The sound of leaves being disturbed, a light, dry shuffle from somewhere high in the branches above them, caught her attention. She looked up. Well, that answered that question. The kitsune was definitely *not* alone. Not that she expected a dragon for its companion. Didn't that just make things a lot more interesting? If her last experience with dragons was anything to go by, then she needed to fly down and draw attention away from the siren. At least until she could convince the kitsune to let the female stay.

Lowering her eyes, she focused on Adoni and pressed a single finger to her lips. *Stay here,* she mouthed. The girl nodded. Good, she understood. Made things easier. Thalasia jumped from the branch and flew into the air, barreling in a nosedive toward the ground. Once she hit about thirty feet from the bottom, she spread her wings and slowed her progress. If she was lucky, the dragon would follow.

And if she wasn't, well... her gaze flicked to the last place she'd spotted the creature. Looked like luck was on her side. Her feet touched the ground with finesse. The kitsune had disappeared during her dive, which meant she got to deal with the dragon. Oh, fun.

Remembering her last encounter, she waited for the leathery thud of the creature landing before raising her hands. "I'm not here to cause problems."

It quickly shifted into human form and he was—naked! Very naked! She averted her eyes but kept her hands in the air. It was the safest bet. It also meant she didn't see the blade until she felt the cold steel kiss her throat. Taking a chance, Thalasia turned her attention back to the male. Thank the gods, a full suit of shiny armor now encased him, glinting under the light.

"Where did you come from?" he asked.

"That's a really broad answer. I mean, I've kind of come from... everywhere really, but if we're talking about in the last few minutes, another realm." Hopefully, she didn't have to explain the term to this guy. She couldn't count the number of times she'd done it in the past. Maybe she needed another more common word to use in its place.

"Are you alone?"

Small favors. The male understood the basic concept of another realm. Or at least knew that other realms existed. Great! One less thing for her to worry about. "Only as much as you are."

"There was another scent. Tell me where they're hiding." He pressed the blade a little harder against her throat, but not enough to pierce her skin.

Not something she could do. But she couldn't exactly say that. "You cut me with that, and I won't be able to tell you anything."

"Stand down, Chase," a feminine voice called out. A female with long, purple hair dressed in a sky-blue kimono with a white belt stepped out from behind a nearby tree. The kimono had an intricate design of cherry blossoms, which complemented both the color of her hair and her dark-red fox-ears.

Chase nodded almost imperceptibly, lowered his hand, and slid the gleaming blade back into the worn leather sheath at his hip.

Okay. Two things. She had a name to put with the male's face, and obviously, the female was the one in charge. Thalasia lowered her hands. "Thank you."

"I didn't do it for you. While I don't sense that you're a threat, I'm also positive you'll be more cooperative this way." The female smiled. "Now. Where is your friend?"

Well, the kitsune had one thing right. She'd be more cooperative without a blade at her neck. The threat part... hmm, that depended on each of their skills. Her last fight with a dragon didn't end badly, but it didn't end well, either. Of course, females fought dirty. "Before we get into all of that, let me verify something. Is this a sanctuary realm?"

"That's a rather specific question," the female replied.

"I know, but's an important one. Everything I've learned about this place says that this is a sanctuary realm. If that's true, then my friend needs sanctuary." Not that she was friends with Adoni, but it was the best way to put it. Better than saying, "This girl I rescued needs a new home."

The female stepped closer, her eyes raking over Thalasia in sharp scrutiny. "You are... unique. I've never seen your particular spirit. What are you?"

Oh, how to answer that? Without giving away details that she simply couldn't. It was the number one rule. She'd broken it once. That was enough. Well, the most believable lie was practically indistinguishable from the truth. "For all intents and purposes, I'm a siren. All you need to know beyond that is that I'm a rescuer. Now, about my friend."

"Mmhmm." Clasping her hands behind her, she walked a slow circle around Thalasia. "Tell me about your friend."

"She's thirteen, a siren, not like me, and..." Her words trailed off. How did she give Adoni's history without going into huge detail? Maybe by using the right word. That was all she needed... the right word. "She's an orphan."

"An orphan?" Chase asked.

Really? He understood realm, but questioned that term? Thalasia frowned. "Yes. She has no family. No one to lean on, and no one who can help her."

The female raised an eyebrow. "Is that why you brought her here?"

"Yes. She needed to be someplace safe. And like I said, everything I know about this place is that it's a sanctuary realm." Although it would've been nice if the notes had mentioned one thing about the kitsune or the dragon. At least she could've better prepared for both if she'd known. Too late now. Something to remember for the future.

"Call your friend. I would like to meet her," the female said.

Alright. This seemed to go in a good direction, or so she hoped. Telepathy would be good in a moment like this, but that wasn't a power she had yet. And probably wouldn't gain for a long time. Not until she met her Allimos. Which meant she had to use alternative means. Thalasia whistled, a low, melodic call that seemed to make the wind itself respond. It was the best she had. Though it would've been great if she could've looked, she didn't want to give Adoni's position away, just in case.

Gods, please don't make me do it again, Thalasia thought to herself. She scrubbed a hand across her gritty face; above, a flurry of leaves rained down as Adoni leaped from the tree. Her lips tugged into a broad smile as she witnessed the show. It kind of amused her. Not that long ago, the young siren appeared to be locked in her shell. This might actually be the best place for her if she reacted like that after just a few minutes.

The three of them watched as Adoni made her way down and slowly landed in front of them. Could the young siren take any longer? It almost amused her to think of the siren as a child. She was only two years older than Adoni. Although she had a lot of mental and emotional years on the girl, so it seemed fitting to think of her as such. Not that she wanted to think about her past too much.

"This is your friend?" the kitsune asked.

"Yes. This is Adoni, and I'm Thalasia." She'd told the kitsune they were both sirens, but the immediate difference between them would be noticeable. Whereas her hair and wings were blue, her companion had long, chestnut hair, and light-brown wings. Not to mention their eyes. While Adoni had another hue of brown, hers were silver. Their only similarity was the feet they each had. Well, so to speak. She had boots and Adoni was completely barefoot.

The kitsune returned to scrutinizing them both and circling them like a predator stalking its prey. She stopped in from of the two of them. "How old are you, Adoni?"

Whatever confidence Adoni had as she leaped from the tree disappeared. The female clung to her arm again before she meekly answered the kitsune's question, "Thirteen."

"Where are you from?"

Oh, shit. She hadn't discussed that question with Adoni beforehand. The girl was likely to answer honestly. Not that it would damage their case at all, but she suspected it would lead to other questions.

"Ba-Ba-Bahalah," Adoni uttered.

"Who did you live with?"

Thalasia sighed, her hand shooting up to silence the inquisition. "She was a child on the run from a cult of warlocks. I rescued her from them, but she couldn't stay in Bahalah in case any of their associates came after her."

Blinking, the kitsune turned her attention to Adoni. "Is this true?"

"Y-ye-yes," the girl got out.

With a small nod, the kitsune clasped her hands in front of her body. "I'm Nira, the Guardhian of this realm." She gestured to herself. "And this is Chase, my Prohtector." Then she gestured to him. "Adoni, you're welcome to stay here." Her gaze flicked to Thalasia. "Are you intending to stay as well?"

"Only for the night. There are others out there that need my help." It had never been the plan for her to stay. But that was a part of the job. The life of an Atlis.

Following along, Adoni looked all around. This realm, as Thalasia had called it, was nothing like Bahalah. There were so many trees. So much fresh air. And so many vibrant colors. She didn't even know how to describe it all.

The ground burst with verdant life, tickling exposed skin with carefree exuberance. It was so squishy. Her gaze lifted from the green blades to the long aisle of bushes with dark-purple flowers on them. She stopped. "Whoa."

"What?" Thalasia asked as she paused in her steps.

A tremor ran through her as she neared the thorny briar, sweat slicking her palm before she dared to grasp for the bloom. The purple lightened at the center and went completely white. Chewing on the inside of her cheek, she hesitantly rubbed the petal between her fingers. It was so soft. Adoni glanced back at Thalasia. "There's so many."

"There are a lot."

The male, Chase, came behind Thalasia and stood there for a moment. "They're called Celestial Midnight."

Thalasia gasped softly, but she saw it, along with the slight jump. Adoni stifled a giggle. Although she'd only spent the day with the female, it hadn't gone unnoticed how much her *friend* hated surprises. Still, given how much she'd always seen her on alert, it amused her that the Chase guy could catch her off-guard. "Are they all this mushy?"

Chase crossed his arms, a faint smile hinting on his face. "Yes. Well, this flower anyway. Not all of them have the same silky texture."

"Wow. I've felt nothing like it." He was nice. Not that she thought Thalasia liked him very much. Although she scowled pretty often. Kind of made it hard to tell. Adoni grinned. "I'm sorry. I didn't mean to slow us down."

"It's okay. New places can do that." He offered her a small nod and started back in the direction they'd been going.

Glancing at Thalasia, Adoni beamed and followed them. She gazed back and forth as they made their way through the long path of Celestial Midnights. While she didn't stop again, she continued to reach out and touch the pretty petals. Although she'd seen other flowers and trees when they first departed the clearing, none of them looked like these.

"We'll be coming to an archway just ahead. Beyond that is where the cabins are located," Nira called from the front of their party.

Adoni leaned in close to Thalasia and whispered, "What's a 'cabin?'" Her throat tightened, and a flush crept up her neck as she considered asking the other two, shame a heavy weight on her tongue. What if they thought less of her? What if they changed their minds and decided she couldn't stay? Where would she go?

"It's a home made entirely of wood."

"Oh." Okay. That made sense. She chewed on the inside of her cheek. Thalasia had said she only planned to stay the one night. What if something like this happened again? And she had another question? There was so little that she knew and understood of the world. Would she be able to ask her new companions? Maybe if she talked to Thalasia, she'd stay longer.

That would be nice. Her eyes lifted as they passed under the archway of vines and flowers, their sparkling surfaces catching the sunlight. Whoa. The farther along they went, the prettier their surroundings got. She really liked this place. She really hoped they didn't come up with a reason to make her leave.

Staring up at the archway, Adoni bumped right into a body. She jumped back and nearly collided with someone else. Her gaze flicked from Thalasia, who'd been behind her, to Chase, who'd been in front of her. "I'm sorry! I'm so sorry! I wasn't watching—"

"Hey, it's okay." Chase held up a hand. "Really, it's okay."

"He's right, Adoni. No harm, no foul. Happens all the time." Thalasia offered her a polite smile.

"Really?" She just hadn't been paying attention. So focused on the beauty that surrounded her; she didn't want them to think she was a klutz. Or that she'd done it on purpose.

"Yes. It's fine," Thalasia said.

"Okay. Okay, thank you." Adoni nodded. *It was fine.* She just had to keep reminding herself of that. New place. New things to learn. New rules. It may take some time, but she would adjust. She'd do whatever it took to stay here.

Thalasia squeezed her shoulder. "Take a look." She gestured forward.

Turning her attention in the direction Thalasia pointed, Adoni gasped. In a large clearing, there were two massive, wooden boxes; the surrounding air smelled of aged wood. One off to the left, and the other off to the right. They looked almost identical to one another. Sunlight poured through crystal-clear surfaces, scattering rainbows across the room. It was really pretty. She liked all the different colors she could see. And there were more bushes of the dark-purple flowers.

"That's the cabin that I live in." Nira pointed to the one on the right. "So, I'll always be nearby. As will Chase. The other one is where you'll live."

Grinning widely, Thalasia gave Adoni's shoulder another firm squeeze. "Would you like to go check out your new home?"

Her eyes widened. "You mean… it's for me?"

"Well, most of those we've given sanctuary to are animals. You're the first person, so yes, that would be accurate," Nira said.

Adoni glanced over at the female with the vibrant hair and a lot of tails. She liked the color of her hair as much as she liked the color of Thalasia's hair. "I can really go look at it?"

"Yes." Nira offered her a faint smile. "In fact, why don't you and Thalasia go look at it together? Chase and I will be in the other one when you're done."

Beaming brightly, Adoni grabbed Thalasia's hand and dragged her toward the big, wooden box they'd given her. Her friend laughed as she pulled her along, and it made her laugh, too.

"Do you think that's such a wise idea?" Chase asked as he crossed his arms. Although he liked the sound of the blue-haired female's laugh, he wasn't certain this spelled anything other than disaster.

"Honestly, I'm not really sure, but I sensed nothing except the truth in what they told us. While I question *how* they got here, we are a sanctuary realm. I cannot turn that girl away." Nira headed down the path that led to her cabin, pebbles crunching beneath her boots.

Really? Had she spoken the truth? He got the feeling that something had been left out of the disclosure. But if Thalasia intended to stay the evening, then it gave him an opportunity to learn more about her. With a shake of his head, he trailed Nira. "Maybe I can talk to her later."

"Figuring out what she hasn't told us isn't your job."

"I know, but... I'm sure I can do more." Words that sounded way too familiar. This was the only place aside from the human world that he'd ever known. All his life he'd been told and taught one thing: how to fight. It wasn't his *job* to ask questions or make assessments. All he had to do was serve as prohtector to the guardhian. In this case, Nira. Though if she died and he still lived, then his duty was automatically passed onto the next guardhian.

She paused with her hand on the knob of the front door and peered over her shoulder at him. "Do you... like her?"

"What? Absolutely not." How would he even know if he did? Maybe he thought she was pretty, but it didn't go beyond that. He knew nothing about Thalasia. Other than he liked her voice and her laugh.

"Don't get attached, Chase. She isn't staying. We are bound to help the girl, not the blue-haired female."

"I know the rules, Nira." Like he could forget. These values had been instilled in him ever since he was named her prohtector, a responsibility he felt in every fiber of his being. It would just be nice to talk to someone new and different.

"Then act like it." Without another word, she opened the door and disappeared inside.

Sighing heavily, Chase glanced back at the other cabin. He could see Thalasia and Adoni walking around through the front windows. The two of them looked like they were having fun, even if the cabin held next to no furniture. Thalasia's radiant smile illuminated the room, reflecting pure elation in its binding glow. He shook his head, another sigh escaping his lips, and forced his feet to move across the worn wooden floor, crossing the cabin's threshold and closing the door behind him with a decisive click.

Thalasia stared for a moment longer as she watched Adoni sleep. It was probably the most peaceful rest the girl had ever gotten. Although she'd rescued her from the warlocks earlier, she was officially safe. No one would ever find her in this realm. With satisfaction settled across her features, she closed the bedroom door most of the way, leaving it open just a crack, and strode down the hallway.

It was a little early for her to rest. The sun had set a few hours ago, but she wasn't exactly tired. Of course, a successful mission often made her a bit more energized than normal. Here it gave her an opportunity to explore just a little. She entered the empty living room and exited through the front door of the cabin. Standing on the small porch, she peered out across the clearing.

She didn't see anybody. She heard only the pleasant chirping, an auditory blanket in the night sky. Lifting her eyes to the thicket looming over the cabins, she stared into the deep-blue darkness, taking a long, slow breath. Quite peaceful. Something Adoni would come to enjoy. Thalasia stepped off the porch and headed around the corner between the two cabins.

"Where do you think you're going?"

"Good gods!" Startled, she jumped, her eyes darting left where Chase was lurking behind the cabin, shrouded in shadows. That was the second time today he'd done this to her. Crikey, she really hated dragons; especially the ones that lurked. When her racing pulse finally slowed, a storm brewed within her, reflected in the burning glare she fixed on him. "I'm going for a walk. Is that okay with you?"

"Do you really think that's wise? Walking around someplace you don't know?"

No, it probably wasn't, but she did it in nearly every realm she ever visited. She tried to use that time to update the map she had of each realm. Something she'd like to do here but likely wouldn't happen. Not with the way the male seemed to watch her. "Only way to learn about a new place is to explore." With a slight grin, she shoved her hands in the pockets of her pants and started forward.

Chase quickly caught up with her, matching her stride. "Are you looking for anything in particular? Or simply keeping it general?"

"General. Like you said, I don't really know my way around. Just figured I'd check some of it out." And leaving him behind didn't really seem to work either. Great. One thing. She'd just wanted to do one thing... maybe she could try again in the morning before anyone got up.

"Alright." Keeping their pace even, he glanced over at her. "What if I showed you something specific?"

Thalasia raised an eyebrow. Why did his question seem like a trick? While they hadn't offered her sanctuary, she hadn't asked for it, either. Not that she would. No place ever really felt like… home. She didn't think she'd ever settle down anywhere. Best she stayed on the move. Safer that way, too. "You'd do that?"

"Yes."

While she was a little wary of the offer, she had little choice at the moment, either. Besides, maybe it would end up being worthwhile to let him take the lead. She shrugged lightly. "Okay. Yeah. Let's do it."

"Perfect." Chase nudged her toward an unmarked path through the forest, splitting off from the dirt one they'd been following.

As they traipsed between tall hedges and climbed over large roots, she noticed he'd changed out of the armor she'd first seen him in. Now, he had on a loose pair of dark pants and a matching shirt. How had she overlooked that? She was pretty good at picking up details… then again, she hadn't noticed him lingering behind the cabin before. Maybe she was losing her touch. Might be something to work on as she continued her travels. "Where exactly are we going?"

He peered over his shoulder and flashed her a brilliant-white smile. "You'll see."

"Why can't you just tell me?" Surprises hadn't ever been something she liked. She preferred to know as much as possible about the realm she was going to, including the different species she might encounter. It made it easier to prepare a persona and exactly what she could display. Or possibly end up fighting. Something that was almost always a possibility. This was one of the few places she had little to go on.

"Because it's something you simply have to see to truly appreciate."

As if that explained everything. Whatever. Whether or not she saw it, she was certain she could appreciate it. There had been a lot of things like that over the years. But this gave her a chance to explore some of the realm. Even if she hadn't been able to do it alone. Up ahead, she spotted a staircase that had been built around the widest and tallest tree she'd ever seen. And she'd seen a variety of them in her lifetime.

Thalasia followed behind Chase as he climbed the stairs, leading them higher and higher until they reached a hollow within the tree. There wasn't a door, really, but it had a rather large, open entrance. Strange. She'd seen nothing like it. Carefully, she ran her fingers along the trim, and it was as smooth as silk.

"Over here." He smiled at her from the other side of the room, which was exactly what it looked like.

A couple of bookshelves lined the walls, complete with books, and several plush blankets littered the floor. Technically, the blankets were all piled in one corner. Shaking her curiosity away, she glanced at Chase. He stood by an open window; the wind whistling softly around an empty frame. It looked almost as if it had been carefully carved and then buffed to a soft sheen. She gave a small shrug before crossing the room, the scent of old books heavy in the air, and peered out the window. "What am I looking at?"

Leaning in close, he pointed toward an extensive field filled with endlessly glowing pink bulbs. No, flowers. Conical-shaped flowers. They were so bright and absolutely stunning. A vibrant color against the backdrop of the dark-blue night sky with a dazzling crescent-moon and sparkling stars that revealed the depths of the universe. A slow smile crossed her face as she glanced back at him. Okay. He had a point. This was something she had to see for herself to appreciate. "What are they?"

"Smoke Blossoms. They look a lot like candy during the day, but at night, they're quite a wondrous sight to behold."

"Yes, they are." Her gaze turned back to the clearing of flowers. It really was one of the best things she'd seen in a while. Not that it explained why he bothered to show it to her. Nor did she intend to ask. Better to believe it was a friendly gesture than to find out he wanted something.

"In all the places you've been, have you ever seen anything like this?"

And there it was... the reason he'd led her there. To find out more information about who and what she was exactly. Well, maybe she could use this to her advantage. "Nope. Can't say that I have. Is that the only field of them?"

"Yes, it's the only place they grow." He glanced over at her. "I figured you might have seen other things that were pretty ... you know...since you've been to a lot of places."

Out of her periphery, she caught him staring. Why was he staring at her? And was there something more to that statement? Nah. He was just talking about the flower. Thalasia shrugged. "I guess I've seen some magnificent views. Of the night sky, setting sun… not that it means every place is like that. Some of them are pretty bleak."

"Oh?"

"Well, yeah. Take Bahalah, for example. It was rather desolate. There was a lot of sand and dry heat there. Not much plant life." All the things that made it difficult to hide as she tried to help defeat the warlocks and rescue Adoni.

His eyebrows knitted together. "That sounds awful. And you travel to these places by yourself?"

And they were done. That probing question caught her off guard, and she wasn't prepared to reveal such personal details on any level. Standing straight, she stared out over the field of Smoke Blossoms. Her mother would've liked something like this. Nope. She wasn't going there. Not tonight. Thalasia shook her head. "I'm getting sleepy. I think I'll head back, but thank you for showing me this."

"Uh… yeah, sure." Chase narrowed his eyes at her.

With a brief nod, she headed for the open doorway they'd come through. Instead of taking the stairs back down, she spread her wings and flew to the ground.

Eleven

There was a knock at the front door. Nira poked her head out of her bedroom, the floorboards creaking beneath her. "Can someone get that?" She hadn't quite finished getting her tails together so she could appropriately hide them. Humans were nosey. Even in the small town of Ogimachi, which was the largest town in Shirakawa Village, the people often stared, and some asked questions.

It had certainly inspired the style they used when they built the two cabins. More specifically, the one she lived in featured a thatched roof over the back half where the bedrooms were, soft and inviting. She had one, Hoshiko had one, and Ahmya had one. They also had one for Chase, but he rarely used it. According to him, sleeping outside was better. Of course, he also required less rest than they did.

"I've got it," Chase called from the foyer up front.

"Thank you," she muttered and returned her attention to her tails. Despite her bedroom being at the very back, she could still hear everything that went on in the house.

The front door creaked open. "Oh, uh, good morning, Thalasia," Chase said.

"Morning, Chase. Is Nira around?"

Hmm... that sounded a little too friendly. Though maybe the female was just being polite. Not that it mattered much. While she still didn't know exactly what the female was, she knew one thing: the female intended to leave today. And that was all that mattered.

"She's in the back getting dressed. You're welcome to come in and wait for her."

"Thank you," Thalasia replied. "I appreciate it."

The front door closed just as she smoothed the last of her tails beneath her kimono, its fabric whispering against her skin. She took a quick glance in the mirror, left the comfort of her bedroom, and strolled down the hall. "I'm right here." Her eyes lifted to the blue-feathered female. "What can I do for you, Thalasia?"

"I wanted to see how I could go about getting the cabin furnished for Adoni. She's not used to having much, but I wanted to make sure it was taken care of before I left."

"Chase and I are going into the market to purchase some basics for her." And she meant basics. A couple of pieces for the front room, along with the major pieces for the bedroom. Kind of a starter set for first-time homeowners.

Thalasia raised an eyebrow. "I didn't know this realm had a market."

"We don't technically, but the human world does." Interesting. The female may have known this was a sanctuary realm, but it seemed her knowledge didn't extend further than that.

"I'm sorry. Say that again?"

"We can access the human world from here." It was actually where most of her tribe lived. The option to live in the realm of An Talamh Lus had been extended over a hundred years ago, but they opted to stay near the farmhouses of the remote town of Ainokura.

The blue-feathered female's silver eyes widened, a silent expression of disbelief. "Okay. Just... uh... make sure Adoni knows that she's never allowed to go into the human world."

"I intended to do that, anyway. As someone who wasn't born here, she wouldn't be able to return to this realm if she did." That wasn't entirely true. It was more difficult and required assistance for her to come back to the realm if she ever left it.

"Good. That's good."

Nira crossed her arms. There was something the female wasn't telling her about the siren, but she didn't think Thalasia would tell her if she asked. Nothing appeared out of place, and she detected no cause for alarm.

Whatever the blue-feathered female was hiding, she had time to figure it out. "Hoshiko and Ahmya are in the kitchen working on breakfast. If you'd like, I can introduce you before Chase and I leave. That way, whenever Adoni awakes, you can do the same."

"Thank you. That would be great."

"Of course, come with me." She led her over to the left and slid open the shoji doors that separated the kitchen and dining area from the rest of the house. At one counter, a female with white wings and bouncy, almond-colored hair stood boiling a kettle of water, preparing cups of tea.

"You are doing it incorrectly," Ahmya, the catalync, said with a flick of her spiked tail.

"I don't recall asking for your opinion," Hoshiko responded over her shoulder.

Folding her hands in front of her, Nira cleared her throat. "Ladies, we have a guest."

"Apologies," the two females replied simultaneously.

Out of the corner of her eye, she caught the smirk that crossed Thalasia's face before it disappeared. "Thalasia, this is Hoshiko and Ahmya. Ladies, this is one of our guests, Thalasia."

"One?" Ahmya asked.

"Yes. Her companion is still resting but will stay here in the realm with us." It was the simplest explanation. Not something she'd entirely shared with them the night before. Despite a fleeting reference.

To her credit, Thalasia offered both of them a small nod in greeting. "It's good to meet you both. Nira, if you don't mind, I'm going to go back and check on Adoni. See if I can rouse her."

"Of course." The sooner she got the siren up and moving, the better. Not to mention, the faster she and Chase got out the door, the sooner the blue-feathered female departed her realm. Something she looked forward to a lot.

"I'll walk her out," Chase said, just as Thalasia turned toward the foyer. Before anyone had the chance to disagree, he was escorting the female out the door.

"That was endearing," Hoshiko commented.

"Not what I would have called it," Ahmya retorted.

"Can the two of you behave yourselves?" Nira's eyebrows pinched together as she stared after the closed door. Despite the accuracy of their statements, she didn't need their arguing or observations bouncing around in her head. She needed answers; not additional problems.

"Where are you going?" Nira asked him.

Chase flashed her a warm smile, his teeth gleaming in the light. They'd collected all the items they needed to bring back in the wagon. While Nira could very well manage the horse on her own, there was something he had to take care of before they headed back. Not that he could tell her that. Or even what he had to do. "I won't be gone long. Just stay here."

Before she had the chance to argue with him further, he walked off toward the back alleys, listening to her call his name the entire time. She'd be fine. No one was going to bother with her, and he wouldn't be gone long. Chase continued deeper into the market's less friendly side, the path becoming more cramped and shadowy. He navigated the alleyways with confidence, each turn familiar and purposeful.

The shop he sought was hidden away, far from the bustling noise of the main path. And he wouldn't have even bothered with this specific item, except one of his questions last night had obviously struck a chord with Thalasia. She'd practically run from the tree when he asked about her traveling alone. It led him to believe one thing: she wasn't alone by choice. Something he understood all too well.

He slowed his pace as he approached the shop that sat in a darkened corner of the dimly lit alleyway. There was no turning back now. Placing his hand on the knob, Chase entered the antiquated building. A bell went off above him, signaling the owner of his arrival. Without wasting time looking around, he strode directly to the counter.

An old man with a long, gray beard and a balding head appeared a moment later. "Can I help you?"

"I need to get a lotus blossom." Most might think he was just purchasing nothing more than a flower, but that wasn't the case. Not with the shaman. No. What he'd selected was an encased flower that repeatedly bloomed, and with the right offering, it allowed the holder to visit lost loved ones in the spiritual plane.

"Understood." The old man bowed his head and turned toward the black case behind him. He retrieved the item Chase sought.

But it wasn't the only thing he wanted. He'd just never asked for anything like what he desired. It was something he'd spent all night thinking about, though. "Is there... something that you have to go with this that will allow me... to watch the holder? When they use it."

It had become quite clear that Thalasia intended to leave today and had no plan to return. Of course, Nira preferred it that way. He, on the other hand, hoped she'd come back one day. Maybe to stay.

"Yes. However, the price is quite steep."

"I've got the funds. Don't worry." He'd pocketed money since he was a hatchling, saving it for a day like today. A day when he really needed it. It wasn't like he wanted for anything else. He'd been taken care of his whole life.

"Very well." The old man grinned. He set down the encased lotus blossom, closed the black case, and walked over to a larger case almost as dark as the first. He removed a crystalline globe from it and returned to the counter. "This will allow you to watch the holder of this lotus blossom. But be careful. The true price may eventually become more than you bargained for."

"Thanks. I'll remember that." He set a stack of cash on the slab of wood, wrapped both of his purchases into a deep-blue, velvet-lined bag, and then tucked them in the folds of his magic. He'd give the flower to Thalasia later.

Thalasia ran her fingers along the jagged wall of the cavern. It had taken some doing, but the cat-like creature and the other winged female had focused enough of their attention on Adoni that she'd been able to sneak out unseen. While she didn't have time to break out her map and scan the realm so she could learn every nook and crevice, she'd at least been given an opportunity to explore without a tagalong.

She found the engravings in the dark mineral intriguing, noting a strange vibration as she ran her fingers over them the deeper she went. And something about them that looked familiar, stirring a faint echo of recognition within her. Not that she could put her finger on it.

This wasn't a realm she'd visited in the past, so theoretically, she shouldn't recognize anything. But honestly, it was like a sense of déjà vu. Like she'd seen these same intricate details somewhere before. But where?

Deeper and deeper sent went, the darkness intensified, and chilling dampness permeated the air. But something drew her in... some invisible force called to her. There were no torches or anything she could've really used as one, not that it impacted her sight at all. Although she saw better in the dark, she wanted to study the rough texture and peculiar details of the crevices in the rocky wall, especially since it seemed impossibly narrow.

Pulling on her powers, her silver magic flowed to her hand and illuminated the immediate area of the cavern. She could've lit the whole damn thing up if she desired, but she didn't want anyone to realize she was in here. Sure enough, she expected whenever Nira and Chase returned, one of them would seek her out.

Thalasia lifted her hand, her fingertips almost brushing the rough stone, and noted the low-hanging ceiling. It had obviously dropped since she first entered the cave. Turning toward her left, she eyed the rigid surface and brought her glowing hand closer to it. The intricate lines were fluorescent, radiating in a beautiful pattern etched into the stygian stone. Wait... there was a space that was hollowed out.

Her eyes widened. She knew why this design looked so familiar. Biting her bottom lip, she untied the strings of her purple purse. It had been passed down through her family, its history spanning several centuries. And it had come in great use over the last few years. Back when it had first been obtained, not only was an extension charm placed on the bag, but a protection one had been as well. It allowed her to carry magical artifacts without anyone knowing. And she definitely had a few.

She searched through the smaller pockets until she found the charm she'd stolen from the enchantress a couple of months back. She beamed as she snatched it from her bag, perfectly aligning the charm with the wall's grooves. In a moment of jubilant discovery, the bright red stone attached to the charm appeared to fit the hollowed-out portion perfectly. How she loved solving a good puzzle!

Now to see what was on the other side. A burst of pure joy radiated from her face as the stone locked in, and she stepped back. The gem glowed, making the light of her hand *really* unnecessary. A tremor vibrated through the space, releasing a show of fine, sandy particles that pattered around her. With her hand shading her eyes from the glare, her gaze snapped to the etched markings. It was... "Uh oh." Her breath hitched, pupils shrinking as her silver eyes grew enormous. She ran toward the front of the cave, gravel crunching beneath her feet, then leaped into the air, flying out in a heartbeat.

Silence had stretched between them as they made their trek back to the realm's entrance. Nira stared out over the fields, still highly annoyed with Chase. When he'd returned, he'd refused to tell her where he'd gone or what he'd obtained. Although she was more than twice his age, she couldn't compel him to tell her. Their roles in their world made them equals. They worked together for the safety of the realm's inhabitants. And yes, she made him run obstacle courses regularly because he still had a lot of training to undergo. In the end, she couldn't force him to do anything.

Gods, she just prayed that whatever he'd picked up had nothing to do with that blue-feathered female. She hadn't even been there a whole day and he seemed way more attached than he should be. Not that it mattered much. The female was leaving in the next few hours, and hopefully afterward he'd forget all about her. It was the last distraction he needed.

Nira kept her eyes forward until they arrived at what looked like an old, weathered barn, standing forlornly in the vast landscape. That design concealed the realm's entrance, making it imperceptible to human eyes. If they saw it from the dirt road, a few miles off, or even turned onto the smaller path that led to the barn... it would appear as nothing more than a dead end. It had worked for centuries. Something she hoped would never change.

Her eyes darted around the bar, taking in every sight and shadow. Something was off. She could feel it in her bones. An icy dread seeped into her marrow, chilling her to the core. No matter which direction she looked, everything about the building seemed normal. Rusty pitchforks still leaned against one wall of dilapidated boards. Empty milk pails sat in the barren stalls. A couple of piles of hay lingered by the open doors. Nothing appeared out of place. It was all as it should be, so why had she gotten this sense that something—unless... Nira sat up straight and turned her attention to the entrance of the realm.

"What's wrong?" Chase asked.

"I don't know, but I feel like... I don't know how to explain it... it's like this buzz that's telling me something has gone awry." Okay. Maybe she knew how to explain it. And whatever it was, they shouldn't have wasted time on his shopping. "We need to move faster."

"I can't just plow through the entrance."

"Yes, you can. Tighten your grip on the reins and give the horse the right command." It sounded really simple, but inevitably he was right. She'd charged into the entrance once when she was younger. It didn't go over very well.

"Have you lost your mind?"

In that moment, it was debatable. She'd given sanctuary to a young siren and knew little about her background. She'd left a blue-feathered unidentified creature with wings—because she was certain Thalasia wasn't a siren—alone with Hoshiko and Ahmya in the hopes they'd monitor her. Her sanity was absolutely questionable. None of that was the point. "Just get us across."

Muttering under his breath, Chase spurred the horse onward, driving it to gallop headlong toward the barn wall, a shimmering illusion. It had been made to look closed with boards nailed haphazardly across, deterring any passersby. Without its rigorous training, the horse likely would have tried to stop, a whinny of protest escaping its throat. Thankfully, the horse continued, and as she expected, Chase pulled on the reins and slowed the wagon to a stop not far into the realm.

Before it had fully stilled, she jumped, her boots crunching on the ground as she landed. Nira had barely made it thirty feet past the entrance when Hoshiko touched down.

"You need to come quick! A drokar has gotten loose!"

"What?" Her jaw tightened, her pupils narrowing into sharp, accusatory points. The damage a drokar could cause. Plus, they weren't exactly the easiest creature in the realm to kill. Hadn't they all been magically sealed in a cave somewhere? How could it have gotten loose? Nira glanced over her shoulder at Chase. "Stay here and guard the entrance. We can't let it get out into the human world."

"Be careful."

Nira gave him a quick nod. Yeah. She was certain the last thing he wanted to explain to anyone was why the Guardhian had died when it was his duty to keep her safe. As quickly as she could, she unwound her tails from under her kimono and focused on Hoshiko. "Show me where it's at."

The female nodded and took to the sky. Nira followed right behind her.

Twelve

Chase sat there in the box of the wagon, staring at Nira as she followed Hoshiko. How did he get stuck with this shit? A low, guttural growl punctuated his grumble. She was punishing him for running off back in the market. It wasn't like he hadn't known where he was going. He used to run around and dart through the back alleys as a hatchling. And he hadn't been gone over twenty, maybe thirty minutes at the most.

Great. He could be useful in finding the drokar and defeating it. Instead, he gets placed on guard duty. Still grumbling, he hopped down from the bench, got the harness off the horse, and settled the creature in its stall. Yeah, because while the drokar was busy setting things on fire and chasing after whatever creatures were nearby for food, it was absolutely going to come this way.

Whatever. He'd be a good prohtector, push the wagon out of the way, and do as he'd been told. Although he could soar after her, even locate the drokar and likely obliterate it with ease, he couldn't abandon the world's entrance, leaving it vulnerable. That would create a disaster that would be beyond repair. Not only would it be bad if humans actually knew beings like him or others existed, but it was also more troublesome for the beings like him that secretly lived in the human world.

There were several that weren't pure enough to stay here in the realm, at least not permanently. Maybe that was why Nira wanted Thalasia to leave so badly. No, that couldn't be it. He didn't get that vibe from her.

From what he could tell, she'd helped that siren out. She seemed like a good person. One he wished he could have known better, sharing laughter and whispered confidences. Once he gave her his gift, he'd be able to observe her closely and learn more about her.

With the wagon out of the way so they didn't lose everything they'd picked up in the village, he scanned his immediate surroundings. Still nothing. Almost as quiet as when they arrived. Chase took a deep breath, filling his lungs with air that smelled clean and crisp for miles. Although he could smell the sweetness of blossoming flowers, along with the fresh scent of dirt, he also caught a rather distinct smell on the wind. The putrid scent of fire. *Shit!* It was a way off, but he could tell the direction it wafted from.

There was no choice.

With a crackle of displaced air and a shower of glittering gold flecks, he shifted into his dragon form, his gaze immediately drawn to the fiery heart of the realm. His snake-like body grew to its massive height and size as gilded scales covered his body. His thick, amber-colored mane matched the color of his eyes. From his location, he could see everything, including Thalasia as she injured the drokar before it darted back into the fray.

He'd never seen such strange magic. It almost looked like... a lightning bolt with no rain. That made no sense. Unless... had she lied?

When the inferno's intense heat stung her face, Nira sent Hoshiko away, urgently instructing the female to get Adoni and Ahmya away from the cabins. The blaze hadn't quite spread that far, but she could hear the crackling embers, and she didn't want to take any chances. Nira scanned the bright, crackling flames as they licked at more of the branches, hungrily devouring any kindling they could reach. Not far off, she spotted a head of blue hair racing between the blazes.

She'd bet anything that female had something to do with the release of the drokar. Only one way to find out. Nira chased after the blue-feathered female, altering her course so the two of them crossed paths. She skidded to a stop before they collided. "Whoa, are you okay? What are you doing?"

"Looking for a two-headed creature with tentacles... or at least I was until you came up."

"The drokar? It went this way?" The female hadn't uttered a word about possibly setting it free, but they could talk about that later. Right now, they had to find it and destroy it before it caused any more destruction. Nira dropped her gaze to the ground and noticed the trail of silver blood leading to the north. Her eyes flicked to Thalasia. "You've wounded it."

"Yeah, I might have done that." Thalasia gestured to the path the creature had left behind. "But I lost sight of it, so I just started following that."

Nira nodded. The story seemed incomplete, with a few gaps that could be filled in later. Normally she tracked creatures with their scent, except the drokar smelled like ash. Mixed in with the smoke billowing around them, it would be difficult to discern. "Alright, let's keep going then. If it's injured, it can't be too far."

"Sounds good."

Together, the two of them took off, using the blood to track it. Hopefully, it led them to the creature's hiding spot.

The blood path they'd followed had ended. Mostly, anyway. Thalasia saw patches here and there, which meant the creature had to be hiding nearby. Right? Thalasia removed the dagger she kept tucked into the waistband of her denim capris. While she'd used her power to tag it before, she couldn't do the same this time around. Not without revealing the truth of what she was to Nira.

And that wasn't something she was prepared to do.

Bearing that in mind, Thalasia squeezed the hilt of the dagger, and it extended in length. The material of the blade strengthened, too. It had been the last gift she'd ever received from her father. One that had served her well over the years. It didn't seem to matter which way she utilized it. Though maybe that was why he'd given it to her.

She scanned her surroundings, hoping to spot more blades of grass glistening with traces of the creature's metallic silver blood. Unlike some supernatural beings, she couldn't follow the magic, either the drokar's—that was what Nira had called it—or her own, even if she'd used it on another. Giving a small nod to the kitsune, they split off. She went in one direction and Nira went in the other. Theoretically, if they met back in the middle, they'd drive the creature out of hiding.

That was exactly what she had expected. It wasn't what happened.

There were a few benefits to being her. Okay, there were a lot of benefits. A lot of things that her particular breeding came equipped with, aside from magic that only grew exponentially with age, included extensive hearing. In her case, it went beyond what any Atlis would have, seeing as she had both dragon and shape-shifter blood running through her veins. Not that she shared those details with anyone.

Still, a noticed the faint rustling of shrubbery behind her. As seamlessly as possible, Thalasia prepared her defense and attack simultaneously. The sound hadn't just come from behind her, but it had also been just slightly above her head. Which likely meant the drokar had perched in a nearby tree. All she had to do—

As the creature leaped at her back, she spun on her heel and swung her sword. The blade of her weapon connected with one of a wet *thwack* against one of its head, slicing it off in one swift maneuver. The wound frothed with silver blood, a repulsive sight that forced her to step back.

"What part of 'don't' did you *not* understand?" Nira yelled across the clearing as she rushed over.

Thalasia blinked. She hadn't heard her say anything. Glancing back, she frowned. The creature was still standing. Why was it still standing? It didn't weave or bob or anything. "This would be a great time to explain."

Taking a firm hold of Thalasia's arm, Nira jerked her backward. "You can't cut off its head. Another will grow in its place."

Yeah, she'd kind of noticed that, especially as the silver blood coagulated and one canine head slowly replaced the other. "You tell me that now?"

"I thought you knew!"

"No! I've never fought a... what'd you call it? A drokar before." Oh, this was bad. Very bad. Even with the wet, splintering crack as a fresh head forced its way out, replacing the severed one, she remained transfixed. The things that should really disturb her... and they didn't. "How do you fucking kill it?"

"You have to—"

Her eyes widened as the creature opened the maw of its other head. She and Nira dove out of the way as the monstrous thing spewed a wave of intense heat and roaring flames in their direction. "Speak faster!" Fuck. They didn't have time for details. Specifics. Thalasia pressed her hand into the ground and jumped to her feet.

"Tentacles! Go for the tentacles! Just don't get hit by one. They're poisonous."

"Good to know," she mumbled. In theory, she might heal herself from it, but it wasn't something she wanted to test out. In case it *didn't* work. Alright. Tentacles. Thalasia leaped behind a tree as a wave of heat washed over her, followed by the whoosh of fire. Crikey. How were they ever going to... oh, she knew how.

Quickly standing, she used the enormous trunk of the tree as cover and glanced at the closest branch. Their best bet would be to come at it from different sides—from above, but they'd have to alternate. Otherwise, they'd give it a chance to escape. Maybe she didn't need to get on the branch. She took a few steps to her right and got the creature in sight again. It seemed to stalk toward Nira.

Perfect! They'd naturally come at it from opposite ends. Keeping her movements slow, steady, and as quiet as possible, she moved behind the drokar. As the creature's lungs audibly expanded, she leaped into the air and slashed at one of its slick tentacles. A loud growl, full of rage, emanated from the drokar as the spindly, black arm fell to the ground with a wet thud. It certainly didn't like that very much. With the aid of her wings, she landed on the other side behind Nira.

It struck at Nira with one of its tentacles, and she swiftly pulled a curved blade from… well she didn't know where it had come from… and sliced it off. There were nine tentacles altogether, and seven remained.

The creature spewed fire at them again, forcing the two of them to split up. They each ducked behind different trees. Okay. There had to be a faster way to do this than cutting those fuckers off one at a time. It would take forever to do that. Unless they came at it as she'd originally thought. "We need to strike from both sides." Or at least something similar. Her gaze narrowed a bit as she glanced between the drokar and Nira. "Both sides… simultaneously."

Nira stared at her for only a second before she nodded. "Alright."

Yeah, it was a little crazy, but it would work. "Draw it away."

The female didn't respond, but the look she shot her way said it all. Nira darted out from behind the tree, gaining the drokar's attention. With a whoosh, several fireballs shot out, setting the surrounding forest ablaze with crackling intensity.

Once she was certain the creature no longer gave her any consideration, Thalasia flew into the air and found the right spot to land. If she and Nira timed it correctly, they'd take out the last of the creature's arms and kill it. And if they didn't… she didn't really want to think about the consequences.

Her eyes met Nira's. They were both in the right position. While Thalasia stood at an angle to the left of the drokar's backside, Nira stood at an angle to the right of the drokar's front side. It was now or never.

She gave the female a nod, and they each charged at the creature, and then leaped into a rolling spin through the air. She went high, while Nira went low. Their blades clashed, sending sparks flying. They each brought their swords down as their feet hit the ground, chopping off a few tentacles in one sweep. Straightening, she spotted one had escaped their attack. Without wasting a second, she threw her weapon at the remaining arm. The tip of her blade skewered it, ripping it from the creature's head, and struck a nearby tree.

The drokar swayed precariously before collapsing with a heavy thud.

Thirteen

Nira eyed the sword that pierced the tree with a tentacle attached to it. She walked a little closer, tilted her head, and focused on the cold, gleaming steel of the blade, studying it more intently. It had some unique qualities to it. It was unlike any weapon she'd ever seen before.

"Well, that was fun," Thalasia said as she yanked the sword and the tentacle out of the tree, the latter of which fell to the ground. "Was it just the tentacles that were poisonous?"

"Um, yes. Though I'd still recommend cleaning the blood off your blade." Spinning on the back of her heel, she strode to where the drokar's body had fallen. She circled the creature. Unfortunately, there wasn't any way to tell who had been responsible for setting it free. While it mattered, she had other things to focus on.

Her gaze turned to the places that had been set ablaze. Slowly, the fires dissipated on their own, which was a good thing. There was still damage to assess, but as long as the inferno died out with its last embers and smoky scent, she didn't have to worry about it spreading and causing further destruction.

"This is a drokar, huh? Never seen one. Didn't even know they existed." Frowning, Thalasia looked back at Nira. "Are they only found here?"

"To my knowledge, yes. Though I'm quite curious how it escaped. These creatures were magically bound to a cave over a hundred years ago."

And she should know. She had bound them. Now that she thought about it, more than one had been restrained, yet there was only one that was seen.

Thalasia dropped her eyes to the ground, scraping at the grass with one of her boots. "Yeah. I might've had something to do with that, but it wasn't on purpose. A total accident, which I'm really sorry about. I didn't think that would happen."

Nira's jaw tightened as she crossed her arms, her gaze fixed on the young, blue-feathered female, a storm brewing behind her eyes. From the moment she'd seen her standing in the middle of that clearing, she'd known the female would be trouble. Although this certainly wasn't the level she'd expected. Either way, it had become quite obvious that leaving her behind with Hoshiko and Ahmya had been a bad idea all around. "You didn't think 'what' would happen? The devastation this creature would leave in its wake, or that killing it wouldn't be as easy as you'd hoped."

A heavy sigh escaped as she kneaded the muscles at the back of her neck. "Well, neither of those really occurred to me. I'd just kind of seen this really neat drawing and paid little attention to what it looked like... until it was kind of too late."

Neat drawing. Didn't pay attention. Now the female sounded like Chase. Not that he'd ever set a drokar loose, even by accident. Nira's jaw clenched as her fingertips dug sharply into her temple, a silent battle against rising fury. "Perhaps next time you'll think about the consequences of your actions before you take them. Now, if you'll excuse me, I need to make sure we destroy the body and that this mess is handled."

"I can help! I mean, since this was kind of my fault, it only makes sense that I stick around to aid with clean-up and the repairs."

"You've done enough. The only thing you need to do is go back to however you got here and leave. Nothing more." First, the female shows up from nowhere, bringing a siren along with her. Second, very few, if any, answers were provided. And now this. A creature that shouldn't have been able to escape to begin with had gotten free. With no actual explanation how it happened, except that it was an accident. Yes, Thalasia needed to go. Now.

Slipping her scimitar back into the folds of her kimono, Nira kneeled by the body. Before she could do anything, her gaze flicked to the far corner of the small expanse. She leaned back on her heels as an immense golden dragon eased to the ground. It shouldn't have surprised her that Chase hadn't listened. She'd left him by the entrance for a reason, but no, he had to make an appearance. Shaking her head, she retrieved a steel dagger from the confines of her attire and quickly cut three symbols into the dirt closest to the drokar.

A silver light emanated from the symbols, slowly encircling the creature's body, humming softly. The luminescence engulfed the drokar, and in a blinding flash, the creature vanished completely. One problem solved. Tucking the dagger away, she rose to her feet and scanned the area for the other problem. Standing to the side, the blue-feathered female was now leaning against a tree, her feathers shimmering in the light. It didn't surprise her that Thalasia had hung around and watched what she'd done. She looked back to where she'd last spotted Chase. He'd transformed into his human guise.

Maybe it was a good thing he'd joined the party. A faint smile touched her lips as he came closer, her eyes softening.

"I know you said not to come, that you could handle it, but I couldn't help myself. Just so you know, I didn't leave the entrance unattended. Hoshiko is watching it."

"Good. That means you can escort our friend here to the clearing where she appeared and make certain she leaves this realm," Nira said. At least *that* he'd be able to do right.

Chase grinned. He almost hadn't believed his luck when Nira told him to walk Thalasia back to... well, the exit, he supposed. Not that Thalasia—either female really—had acted all that enthusiastic about it. Either way, it gave him the perfect opportunity to give her the lotus blossom he'd picked up. He just had to find the right moment. "So, can I ask you something?"

"Sure. Just don't be surprised if I don't answer."

He kind of hoped she did. While he didn't plan to tell Nira about what he'd seen, an explanation would be nice. "I saw something earlier when I was guarding the entrance in my dragon form. We have great eyesight, you know?"

"And excellent hearing, but I doubt that's your question."

So, she knew about dragons, huh? How much did she know? And how did she know? Obviously, she wasn't a dragon herself, but it certainly raised a few questions. "You were chasing after the drokar, and I saw... well... it kind of looked like lightning."

Thalasia stopped mid-step, and her silver gaze shifted to him. "No idea what you're talking about."

"I will tell no one if that's what you're worried about. I'm just... curious." His curiosity piqued, yet he restrained himself. Throughout his life, he experienced the feel of countless unique magical energies. Nira's celestial, plus elemental magic within the tribe, and then what he knew of his own magic. But he'd seen nothing like what Thalasia had done.

Her knuckles whitened as she massaged her neck, a frustrated sigh escaping her lips. "No one was supposed to see that," she muttered.

"I'm great with secrets. I promise, you can tell me, and it'll stay with me forever." That was the complete truth. He really hoped she saw that in him. Maybe she couldn't stay, but they could be friends, right? Friends who didn't talk or spend time together, but friends.

"Look, it's ... complicated. The most I can tell you is that, obviously, I'm not a siren. I'm, special, unique... one of a kind." Thalasia paused. "You get the picture."

His eyes twinkled as his head gave a slight, eager dip, a spark of excitement bubbling within. "I know all about that. I'm the only dragon-shifter in this realm. My people, we used to live in the village... in the human world. I'm not positive of the details, but from what I was told, all the dragon-shifters were destroyed. I was still in an egg, and somehow, I survived. Nira's tribe... well, one tribe, anyway, took me in. They helped me hatch and have been taking care of me ever since."

One thing he'd learned over the years was that if you skipped the specifics, people didn't look at it too closely. Instead, they focused on the broader truth. Not that he didn't trust her, but he didn't want her to pity him, either. He just wanted her to relate to him. Not that he could explain why.

"I'm sorry to hear that, Chase. I know how lonely you must feel." Pausing, she bit her bottom lip. "My parents... they, uh... they died a few years ago. I don't... I don't really talk about what happened."

His eyebrows knitted together. She didn't talk about it? Did that mean... it had to... that was the only thing that made sense. Someone killed her parents. He understood that all too well. Although it sounded as if she'd gotten time with them. "Sounds like you miss them a lot."

"All the time," she mumbled, her voice cracking with sorrow as she turned away.

He stared at her for a moment. When they'd been up in his tree, he'd only suspected it, but right then, he could see it for sure. She was lonely. Propelled forward by his speed, he quickly caught up with her. "If you had the chance to talk to them, to see them, would you take it?"

"In a heartbeat."

"Maybe I can help with that." The words had come out of his mouth before he could stop them. He'd meant to lead into it slowly, to get to know her a little more, but obviously his head had other ideas.

Thalasia halted in her steps again, and her eyes flicked in his direction.

For a split second, her gaze had softened. In that moment, he wanted to kiss her. Which was a bad idea. A *terrible* idea, especially if the way she narrowed her eyes at him was anything to go by. But he could give her the gift he'd obtained for her. Chase reached into the folds of his kimono and retrieved the encased lotus blossom. His face held a faint smile as he offered it to her with a quiet flourish.

Lifting her gaze to his, she blinked. "What's this?"

"It's a lotus blossom. It allows the user to transport to the spiritual plane, where they can communicate with lost loved ones." There was more to it, more details he needed to give her, but he wanted to see if she would accept it first.

"And it's for me?"

"Yes." His face blossomed with pure delight. "I wasn't positive, but I'd gotten the sense last night that you'd lost someone special to you. So, I got one for you."

She stared at him for a long moment. Hesitantly, she held out her hand. Chase's smile grew, lighting up his eyes as he placed the flower in her palms. She'd done exactly as he'd hoped. He gestured to opening at the top of the encasement "When you want to use it, you'll prick your finger and squeeze a few droplets of blood here. Then set it in your lap and meditate. It'll create a bubble around you for as long as you're in the spiritual plane."

"I... uh... I don't really know what to say about this." Thalasia looked from his intense stare to the precious artifact she clasped "Thank you. Really, thank you."

"You're quite welcome." It thrilled him to no end that she'd accepted his gift without question. This couldn't have gone better if he'd planned every detail out.

Without another word, she untied the purple bag attached to her pants, and the lotus blossom disappeared inside of it. Wasn't that interesting? Must have an extension charm or something on it. It certainly didn't look like the flower was tucked away inside of it.

With a sharp tug, she secured the purse strings in a knot, then fastened the bag to her pants, offering him a ghost of a smile. Thalasia opened her mouth—her eyes rolled into the back of her head and her entire body went lax.

Chase caught her, his strong grip halting her fall just before she hit the hard ground. "Thalasia? Thalasia?" He got no response from her. No words, no sounds... nothing.

Standing on a white sandy beach, Thalasia glanced across the deep-blue crashing waves. The rippling of the water increased as small boats approached from either side of the rainbow bridge, each filled with strangely deformed humanoid creatures. They weren't alone. Merfolk in striking armor wielding tridents and dragons crawling along the rising tide all approached from a variety of angles.

"Focus on your place. We'll deal with them."

"What're you doing?" a female voice asked from behind her.

Her gaze narrowed at the siren. "I thought I told you to stay away from here! You're too valuable."

"It'll take everyone doing their part. While I won't fight, you need power, and a lot of it."

"I can't do anything until I have the last string." Her hand settled on the hilt of the sword sheathed at her side. She lifted her eyes toward the sky, but the rays of the sun blinded her from anything that might come from above. Turning her attention back to the land, she looked first to her right, and then to her left. A multitude of species stood alongside her... Seelie, shape shifters, dryads, nymphs, chimeras, dwarves, trolls, and more.

They had all joined together for an epic battle.

Thalasia gasped, blinking rapidly as the blur of green above her slowly came into focus. But that wasn't the cold, hard ground she felt beneath her wings. No, it was an arm, and there was another under her knees. Flicking her gaze toward a face she still couldn't quite make out, all she could see was a strong, angular jaw. Not that she cared who had a hold of her. "Put me down now."

"Okay. I can do that." Gently releasing her, Chase lowered her feet to the soft grass.

As she got situated and steady on her own two feet, her surroundings finally became clear. Shit. She hadn't meant for that to happen. Not like she could've stopped it, though. Damn things did what they wanted when they wanted. Thalasia glanced around to gather her bearings. Right. They'd been walking through the forest toward the jump point. She peered over her shoulder in the opposite direction.

Large, knobby roots protruded from the earth. Thickets of multicolored fallen leaves covered the dry blades of grass. The wind whistled around the trunks, ruffling the greenery that had yet to change their hue or float to the ground. Not far off from where they stood, she spotted the bright purple that engulfed them upon their arrival. A sweet scent wafted through the air.

There was definitely no beach. Not that it was any place she recognized. Nor had she known any of the faces she'd seen. She turned her gaze to Chase, his brow furrowed in a worried expression as his eyes remained fixed on her. Shit. Shit. This was one of the many things she tried very hard to keep to herself. Obviously, the universe had other ideas.

"Are you alright?"

Thalasia's breath hitched, a cold weight pressing down on her chest. That depended on his definition. Most times, she definitely wasn't alright, but she was still alive. "I'm fine."

"Good. Now, what just happened?"

"Aside from the obvious?" It was a dumb question, and yet she'd asked it anyway. She didn't need to see him nod to know he preferred details, or at least some kind of valid explanation of why they were talking one minute and the next she appeared to black out. Thalasia gestured in the direction they needed to go. "Can we walk and talk?"

"As long as you answer my questions, yes."

"I promise... I'll give you answers." The best she could went unsaid, but she wasn't positive if he understood that or not. His consent echoed in her mind, a hollow sound as she trudged ahead. "I told you, I'm unique. Well, I have visions. They typically lead me to other realms across the universe."

"So, when you passed out, you were really just having a vision?"

"Yes." What the vision meant, well, that was something she'd have to figure out. Along with when it was supposed to take place and where it would all go down. Ah, yes, the life of an Atlis. It was like one long, massive fucking puzzle that never ended. Yeah, being her came with perks and responsibilities. A lot of responsibilities.

"Will you tell me what you saw?"

"No." She smirked at the glare he shot her. "Look, I said I would give you answers. I didn't say I'd give you the answers you wanted."

"Fair enough," Chase said. "I just don't understand why you can't tell me."

The simplest explanation... she didn't want to, but that probably wouldn't go over well. And he had just given her a pretty amazing gift. One that she hoped really worked. Being able to talk to her parents again, either to talk, or even if they intended to chastise her for the studying she hadn't continued, she didn't care. As long as she got to hear either her mother or father's voice.

Her thoughts had completely trailed off-topic. She needed a good way to respond. Something that would appease him and not make her seem like a bitch simultaneously. Hmm... that might work. "The visions are complicated. I get a brief glimpse of time and space. I can't really say what it is until I put all the pieces together."

"You mean you might get multiple visions, and they're all related to each other in some way?"

"Yeah, exactly." Which meant this was the first vision of likely a long line of them to come. Especially if it ended in some kind of massive battle. Somewhere where several different species cohabitated. Although with a fight like that, it may not be peaceful.

"Okay. Was this the first or have you had similar ones before?"

"I've seen nothing like this before." That didn't mean she hadn't fought other creatures before. Echoes of fights past clung to her, but this... a wave of cold washed over her as the suppressed memory threatened to drown her. Yeah, there hadn't been one like that before.

"Are you alright?"

"I'm fine," she replied automatically. Too much had already been said regarding anything involving what she was and everything that included. Her gaze lifted as they approached the clearing. Thank the gods. She'd never been more ready to end a conversation.

"Alright. Just asking." Chase nodded toward the expanse. "I guess we're almost there."

She hadn't intended to come off snippy, but sometimes it simply came out that way. Taking a fortifying breath, she ran her hand over her hair. "I apologize if I was rude. I'm just... not very good at talking about myself."

"I understand."

Yeah, that was probably the truth. Her eyes flicked toward the jump point. Not that he could see the spiritual markings that she could. Now that she thought of it, though, it surprised her the kitsune couldn't see it. Then again, maybe Nira had seen it and simply monitored it. Were there other beings that could see them? Something to think about. Thalasia looked back at Chase. "Thank you again for the flower. And for taking Adoni in. Just... like I said earlier, please, please make sure she doesn't traverse into the human world."

"Nira will make certain she knows." He offered her a smile, a gentle curve of his lips. "And you're welcome. Be safe, Thalasia."

All she could do was nod. For an Atlis, safety was an illusion. There wasn't any place in the universe where she'd truly be safe. Stepping into the center of the clearing, she untucked the lyre from her tank top and ran her fingers across the strings to rearrange the spiritual emblems. Then, she placed the first two fingers of her right hand together in the north position and moved them in a circular motion. A rainbow of colors sparked to life, opening the gateway, which she stepped through, leaving the realm of An Talamh Lus behind.

Several minutes had passed since the air had rippled with a visible, silent wave. Although she hadn't seen the blue-feathered female leave, the weight that her presence had placed on her shoulders had completely disappeared. It could mean only one thing.

"Thalasia has left," Chase said.

"Good." It shouldn't have made her as happy as it did, but she hated when things weren't running smoothly in her realm. Her tails flicked back and forth. Nira peered over her shoulder at her prohtector. "What? Why are you giving me that look?"

"I'm just trying to figure out if you really think she was all that bad."

"Have you seen the destruction that was caused because she *accidentally* let a drokar loose?" Not that it was as bad as it could've been. After she'd flown through the charred remains of the forest and taken it all in, it appeared they'd killed the drokar before more harm could be done. Most of the animals within the realm had escaped the creature's maw, and even more had gotten to safety before the blaze swallowed them whole. That they'd been able to kill it quickly and it had been unsuccessful in feeding seemed to be the only reasons the damage was less than initially believed.

"Yes, I have. And you're making a big deal about it. Granted, she shouldn't have been exploring the realm to begin with, but I don't imagine you expected her to stay put."

"No, I didn't. Just like you did exactly what I told you not to do." Although hopefully with the female gone, this was the last she would hear of it. Whatever attachment he'd developed would disappear, and things would return to normal, just with a new addition.

"I did nothing."

Nira gave him a sharp, irritated look. She would not argue with him about it. No one would win a fight like that. Instead, it was better for them to focus on what needed to be done to repair the wreckage. "I need to round up all the animals, make sure we've found all of those that were injured, and take them back to the stables. While you do that, I'm going to make sure our new friend knows the fundamental rule around here... and see how we can involve her with the restoration of this area."

"Fine," Chase grumbled. He spun on his heel, the leather of his boots squeaking, and paused mid-step. "Thalasia asked that we make certain Adoni doesn't go into the human world."

Frowning, she raised an eyebrow. That was something she'd do anyway, but that was the second time the blue-feathered female had made that request. Why? Nira's gaze turned toward the cabins.

What exactly had she agreed to by allowing the young siren to stay? Uncertainty tightened its grip, each unanswered question a tightening knot in her chest, threatening to suffocate her. Perhaps in the days ahead, she could desperately piece it all together.

After all, time was on her side.

Or so she believed.

To Be Continued
In
Jail Break
The Atlis Chronicles

Book Two

About the author

ABOUT THE AUTHOR

Krys Fenner, also known as **Brigit Rosé**—like the wine, not the flower—has been infinitely passionate about writing and helping people for as long as she can remember. Having already published nine books, she avidly works on multiple series, from social issues to paranormal romance. While she loves everything she writes, she's genuinely excited about the other series she'll co-authors over the coming year. Krys received an Associate of Arts in Psychology, a Bachelor of Arts in Creative Writing, and is currently working on a Master's degree. When she isn't writing, she's spending time with her three fur babies, Bones, Luna, and Lola. To learn more about Krys Fenner and her upcoming book releases, visit her official website: https://kbfennerrose.com.

Also by Krys Fenner

Also by Brigit Rosé

ALSO BY BRIGIT ROSÉ
Love's Worth Series
UnHinged
ReIgnited
The Mystic Chronicles
Detached
The Lucent Chronicles
Grace's Beast
Shattered Wonderland
The Arcarean Academy
Wicked Ground

Co-Authored

CO-AUTHORED
Prisma Isle Series
Perfectly Reckless
Chaotic Tranquility
Rebel Tides

Coming Soon

COMING SOON
Betrayed (Dark Road Series)
ReUnited (Love's Worth Series)
Inherited (The Guardhian Series)
Siren's Curse (Prisma Isle Series)
Silencing the Shape Shifter (Prisma Isle Series)
Kingdom of Embers (Prisma Isle Series)
Savage Ground (The Arcarean Academy)
Consumed (The Mystic Chronicles)
Dark Entanglement (The Midnight Chronicles)
Jail Break (The Atlis Chronicles)
Blood & Bondage (The Empyreal Den Chronicles)

www.ingramcontent.com/pod-product-compliance
Lightning Source LLC
Chambersburg PA
CBHW070511200726
48293CB00007B/2486

* 9 7 8 1 9 5 5 1 0 6 4 6 7 *